BACKSTORIES

DC COMICS

SUPERMAN™

THE MAN OF TOMORROW

By Daniel Wallace

Illustrated by Patrick Spaziante

Superman created by Jerry Siegel and Joe Shuster

By special arrangement with the Jerry Siegel family

SCHOLASTIC INC.

All rights reserved. Published by Scholastic Inc., *Publishers since 1920*. SCHOLASTIC and associated logos are trademarks and/or registered trademarks of Scholastic Inc.

The publisher does not have any control over and does not assume any responsibility for author or third-party websites or their content.

This book is a work of fiction. Names, characters, places, and incidents are either the product of the author's imagination or are used fictitiously, and any resemblance to actual persons, living or dead, business establishments, events, or locales is entirely coincidental.

ISBN 978-0-545-86818-1

10 9 8 7 6 5 4 3 2 1   16 17 18 19 20

Printed in the U.S.A.   40
First printing 2016

Book design by Rick DeMonico

Thank you to Michael Regan, George Corsillo, Jerry Ordway, and Matthew Manning for their additional contributions to the artwork in this book.

CONTENTS

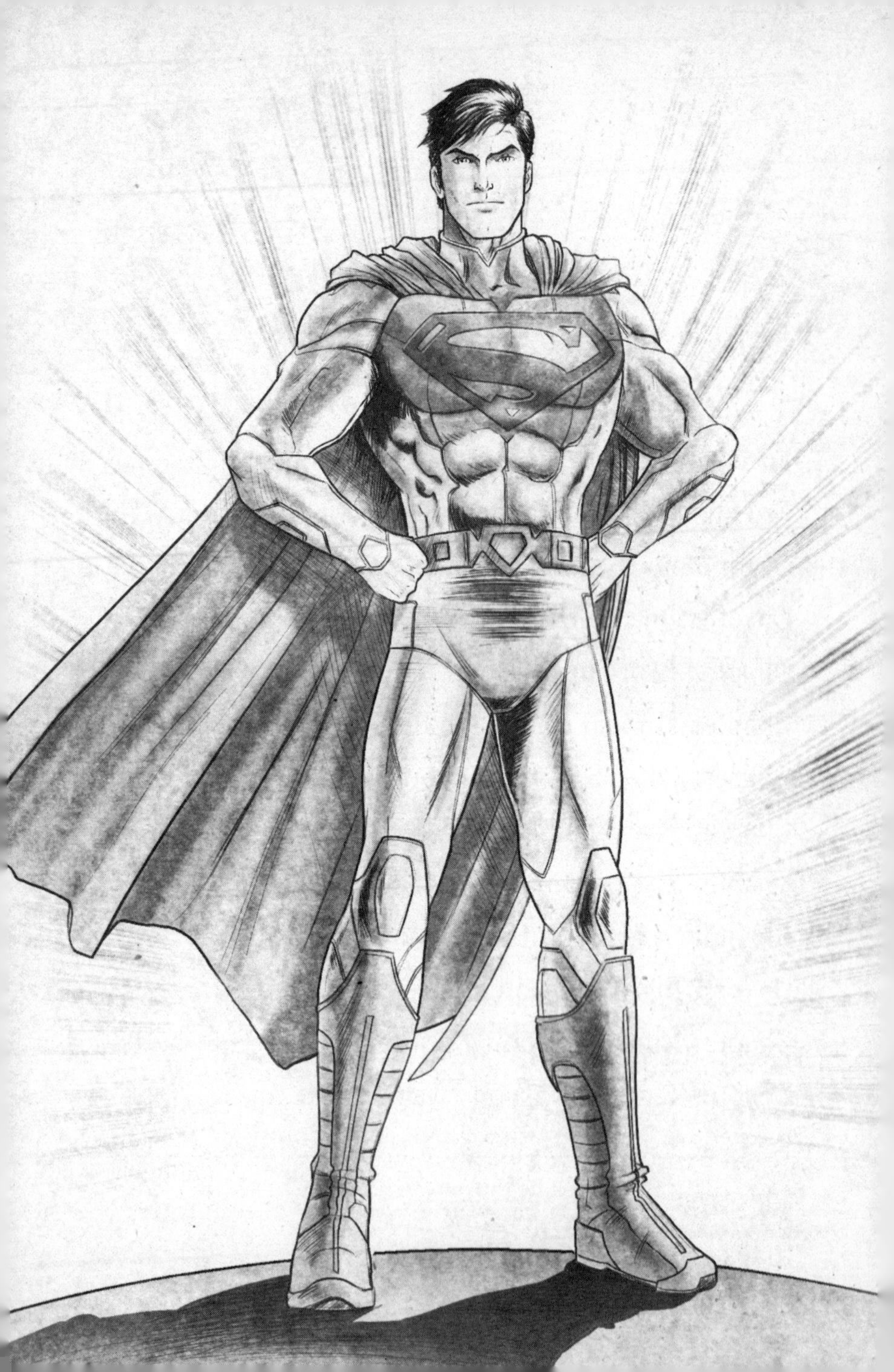

Foreword
by Superman

If you knew me when I was a kid, you would never have called me "super." I grew up in a little farming town that most people have never heard of. I definitely wasn't stronger or better at sports than most kids my age. But for as long as I can remember, I always wanted to help people.

Some people I saw, like firefighters or police officers, took a hands-on approach—they stopped crimes and rescued families. Others helped in different ways, reporting on important events or inventing new devices. While I tried to figure out what I wanted to do with my life, my parents always encouraged me. They never told me that something couldn't be done, and if I failed they urged me to try again. I had no doubt that I would help people—but I was shocked when I learned *how*!

I started to develop superpowers as I grew up. Powers like incredible strength, unbreakable skin, heat beams that shot from my eyes, and even flight! It scared me at first, but then I discovered that I had been born on another planet. My abilities were normal (well, normal for a Kryptonian living on the planet Earth), and they didn't make my adoptive parents love me any less.

I knew then that I couldn't waste these gifts. I started using my powers to help others, and became the world's most famous Super Hero.

But that didn't stop me from improving my other skills as Clark Kent. I studied hard, and I got a job at a newspaper in Metropolis. As a reporter for the *Daily Planet*, I could reveal the truth about what corrupt and powerful people were *really* doing.

I became good friends with my coworkers. People like Jimmy Olsen and Lois Lane showed me that everyone can make a difference for the better.

I am happy that I've been an inspiration to other Super Heroes, and I am proud to join them in the fight against injustice. If danger threatens the innocent, I will be there.

Friends, Foes, and Family

Superman

He was born on Krypton, but sent to Earth as a baby, where he was adopted and named Clark Kent. Upon discovering his history and superpowers he decided to use his gifts to help others. In doing so became known as Superman.

Jonathan and Martha Kent

Superman's adoptive parents. They raised him in the farming town of Smallville as their son, Clark Kent. Jonathan and Martha gave Superman the values of hard work and honesty.

Jor-El and Lara

Superman's Kryptonian parents. When they realized their home planet would explode, they sent their son, Kal-El, to Earth, knowing he would gain powers under a yellow sun.

Lana Lang

Clark Kent's best friend during his childhood in Smallville. Lana was one of the only people in town who knew that Clark could do amazing things.

Lex Luthor

A genius, and one of the wealthiest people in Metropolis. Clark and Lex knew each other back in Smallville but Lex later became Superman's greatest enemy.

Perry White

The editor in chief of the
Daily Planet newspaper.
Perry, who has worked in
the news industry all his life,
made the decision to hire
Clark Kent.

Jimmy Olsen

The *Daily Planet*'s junior
photographer. Jimmy is
Superman's friend, and
he wears a watch to alert
Superman if he is ever in
danger.

Lois Lane

The *Daily Planet*'s top
investigative reporter. Lois
and Clark are coworkers.

Metallo

A Kryptonite-powered super-villain. Lex Luthor created Metallo by equipping soldier John Corben with mechanical parts.

General Zod

A Kryptonian criminal who escaped from the Phantom Zone. General Zod is a ruthless fighter who has all the same powers as Superman.

Supergirl

The second Kryptonian hero to appear on Earth, also known as Kara Zor-El. Superman and Supergirl are cousins.

Chronology

Two Kryptonian parents, Jor-El and Lara, place their baby, Kal-El, into a rocket and send him away before their planet explodes.

The rocket lands in Smallville, Kansas. A farming couple, Jonathan and Martha Kent, raise the baby as their son, Clark Kent.

As Clark grows up he starts to develop strange powers, including super-strength and heat vision.

Clark meets the time-traveling Legion of Super-Heroes and wears his famous costume for the first time.

After graduating from Smallville High School, Clark studies journalism at college.

Clark gets a job as a reporter at Metropolis's *Daily Planet* newspaper, and meets Lois Lane and Jimmy Olsen.

When more Super Heroes appear, Superman unites them into a team called the Justice League.

Another survivor of Krypton, Kara Zor-El, arrives on Earth and becomes Supergirl.

Superman builds a secret base called the Fortress of Solitude in the frozen Arctic.

Clark's parents show him the rocket that brought him to Earth. Clark learns he is a Kryptonian.

Clark meets a very smart boy named Lex Luthor, but he can't convince Lex to be his friend.

While saving his friend Lana Lang from a tornado, Clark discovers he can fly.

In his costume, Clark saves Lois from falling off a building, revealing his superpowers to the world.

The *Daily Planet* runs a front-page story about the new hero and gives him the name "Superman."

Superman fights Metallo, an enemy who uses Kryptonite to weaken him.

General Zod, Brainiac, and other enemies threaten humanity, but Superman defends the world from their menace.

CHAPTER ONE

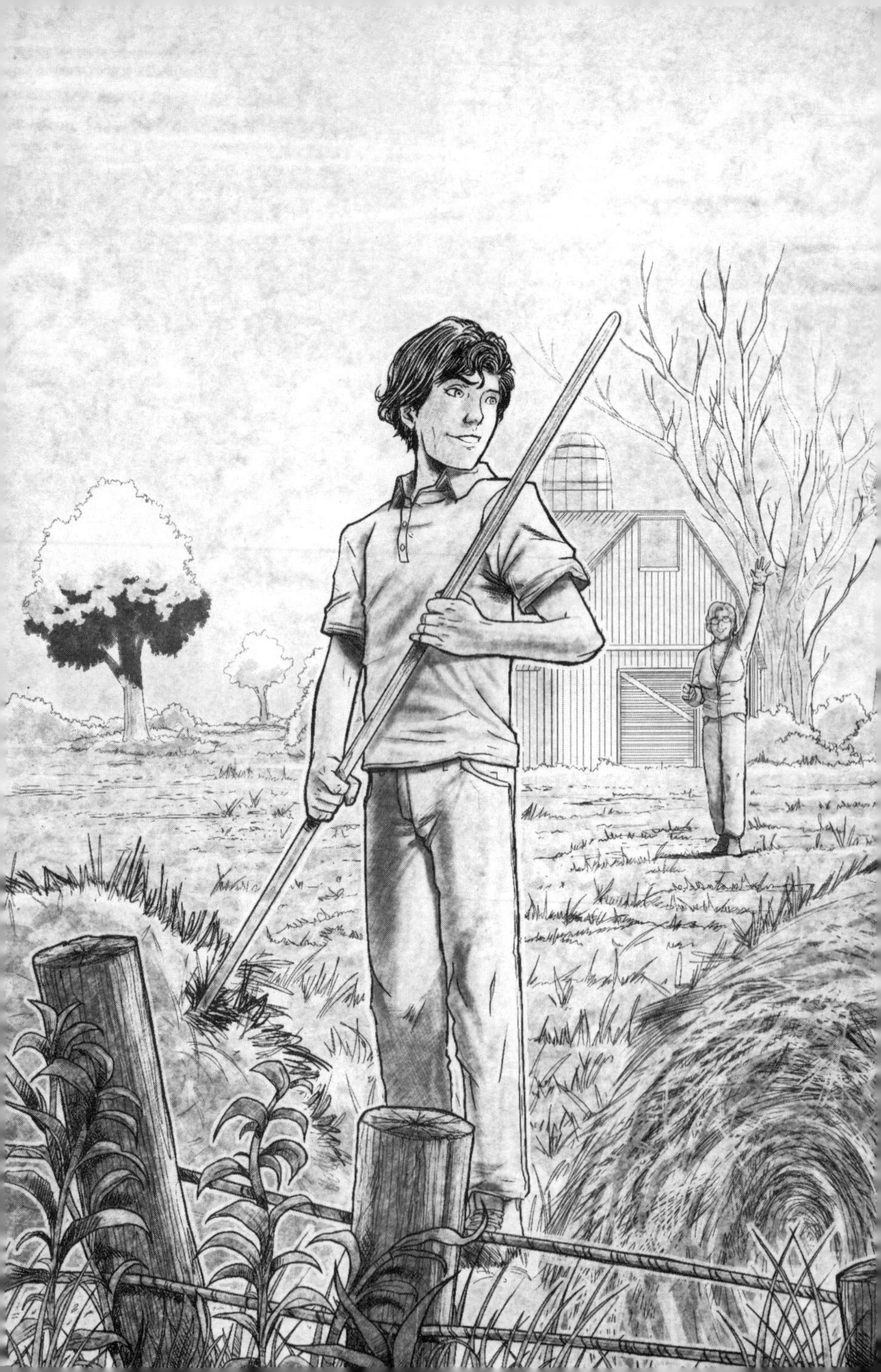

THE KID FROM SMALLVILLE

Smallville, Kansas, was an ordinary American town, and Clark Kent seemed like an ordinary American boy. Clark, who had no brothers or sisters, lived on a farm with his parents. He went to school, did chores, and played with his friends.

But Clark was not ordinary. Even at a very young age, he could do things that no other child his age could do. Once while helping his father repair a tractor, he lifted the front end off the ground with only one hand. Another time, during one birthday

party, he blew out his candles so hard that the cake sprayed all over the kitchen wall.

Clark's parents, Jonathan and Martha Kent, had lived in Smallville all their lives. Everyone in town knew that the Kents wanted a baby, so it was a happy day when Martha appeared in town carrying a newborn son. During the years that followed, Clark grew up believing that Jonathan and Martha were his natural mother and father.

The Kent farm had been in their family for generations. It wasn't large—just a house, a barn, and several acres of cropland—but it took a lot of hard work to take care of it. Clark had to fix equipment, till the soil, organize the toolshed, and more. The Kents weren't rich, but they were happy.

A BRONZE CASTING OF BABY CLARK'S HANDPRINT.

Whenever Clark did something out of the ordinary, his mother and father looked worried. They seemed to be waiting for something to happen, but they never told Clark that there was anything different about him. Clark started to wonder why he wasn't like the other kids and whether his strange feats of strength—like the time he hit a baseball so hard it

17

disappeared into the clouds—would end as he got older.

Lana Lang was a girl about Clark's age, and she was one of his best friends in Smallville. Clark felt

MARTHA, JONATHAN, AND CLARK KENT ON THEIR FARM.

My Hero by clark kent.

My Hero is my pa Jonathan kent. when I grow up I want to be as strong as him and as good at handeling problems like when Mrs. summers got sick and he mowed her yard for her and and did not even ask for any mony. He also lets me stay up late when mom goes to kansas city to visit uncle Bert. I would not trade my pa for any dad in the whole universe

A YOUNG CLARK'S SCHOOL ESSAY, AN ODE TO HIS FATHER.

Jonathan and Martha Kent, and their farm

The land on which the Kent farm is located has been owned by multiple generations of the Kent family going all the way back to the 1800s. Jonathan Kent is proud of his family's legacy, but he doesn't have much money to modernize or expand the farm. Most of the work for cultivating and harvesting crops is done by Jonathan, Martha, and their son, Clark, using old tractors and other pieces of farming equipment.

comfortable whenever he talked to Lana. On the condition that she would not tell anyone else, he revealed all of his experiences.

One day, Clark and Lana were playing hide-and-seek in a cornfield near the Kent farm. Lana crouched down in the middle of the tall cornstalks, waiting for Clark to find her, not noticing the

SMALLVILLE IS LOCATED IN THE HEART OF KANSAS, IN THE MIDWEST REGION OF THE UNITED STATES. ITS PRIMARY INDUSTRY IS FARMING.

CLARK DOESN'T FEEL THE BLADES OF THE THRESHER!

approaching threshing machine. At the last instant, Clark stepped in—shielding Lana from the thresher with his back. The machine's sharp blades tore Clark's shirt, but didn't leave a single scratch on his skin. Lana was amazed and relieved. Clark felt like a hero!

When Clark started high school, the changes came even faster. One weekend, Clark and his friend Pete Ross played a game of football. When Clark knocked Pete to the ground, his friend shouted in pain. Clark had broken his arm!

No one blamed Clark for the accident, but Clark knew that he needed to be more careful around others. His special abilities had the power to hurt people.

At school the next week, Pete Ross proudly showed off his arm cast to everyone in the hallway. Clark stared at the cast, trying to read the signatures of his classmates who had already signed it. Instead, he saw right through the cast—all the way down to Pete's broken bone!

Scared and confused by what he had just seen, Clark ran away into a quiet corner of the school. Lana, who had seen what had happened, found him

CLARK IS SCARED WHEN HE SEES PETE ROSS'S BONE.

there and helped him calm down. As the two friends talked, they opened up about their feelings for each other. Lana leaned in to give Clark a kiss.

His emotions in a whirl, Clark tried to say something. Suddenly, out of nowhere, energy shot from Clark's eyes! Two beams of light streaked past Lana, hitting the wall and setting a Smallville High banner on fire. Upset by the accidental damage he had caused, a dejected Clark watched in silence as firefighters arrived. The school's principal thought that someone had tried a dangerous prank.

Clark told his parents what had happened. Jonathan and Martha Kent listened to their son's fears, their hearts breaking when they heard how unhappy he was at being so different from all the other kids.

They decided the time had finally come to tell Clark the truth.

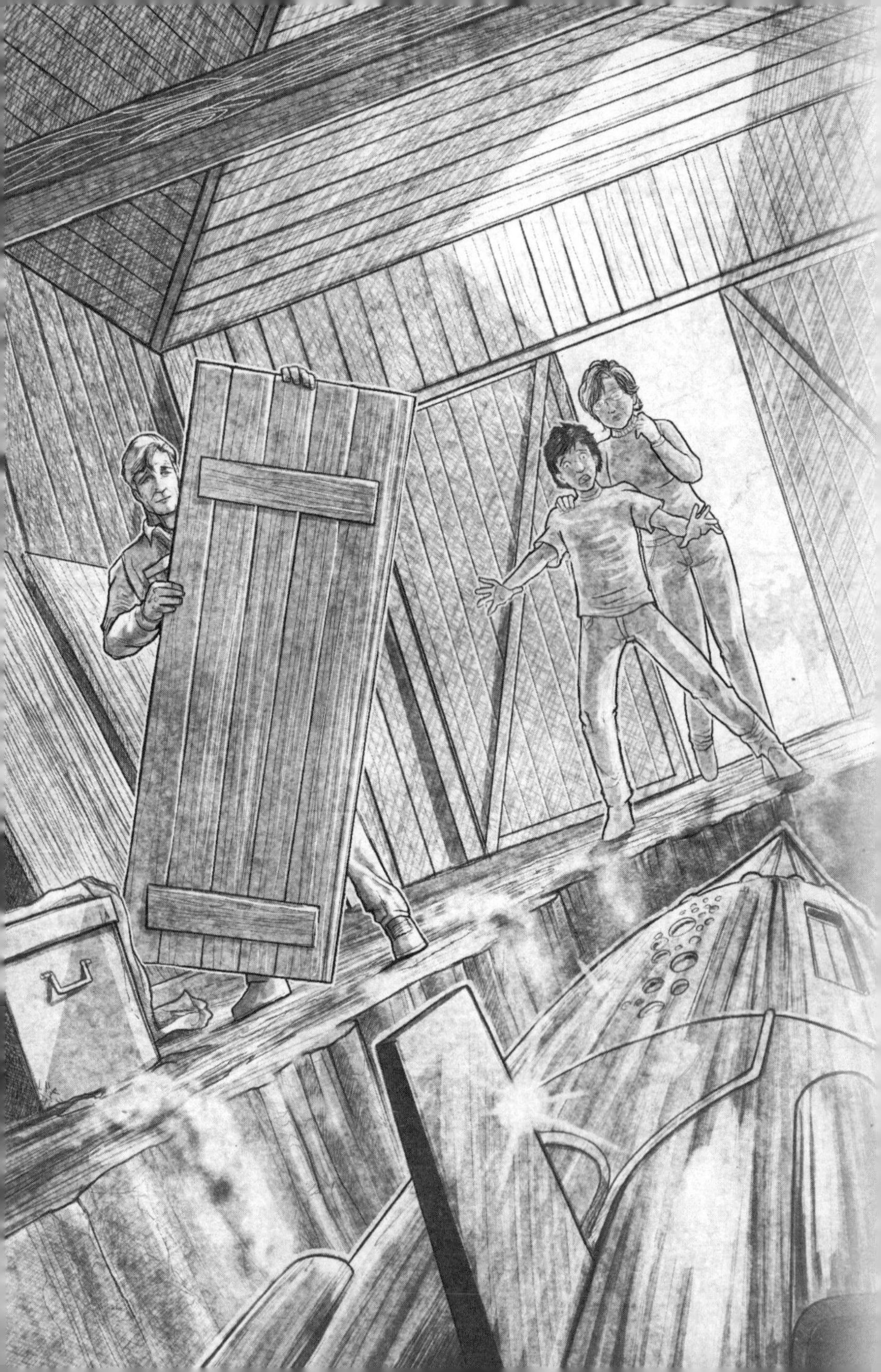

CHAPTER TWO

THE WORLD OF KRYPTON

Clark had been in the dusty barn hundreds of times while doing his chores, but this time something was different. His mother and father led the way and then closed the barn door for privacy. Clark's father dragged aside a tarp on the floor, uncovering a hidden door. With a firm tug on the handle, the door creaked open. Clark couldn't believe what he saw inside.

A *spaceship*. That was the only word that fit. The pointed shape and directional fins on the strange

A DIAGRAM OF JOR-EL'S COMPLETE ROCKET SHIP THAT CARRIED KAL-EL TO EARTH.

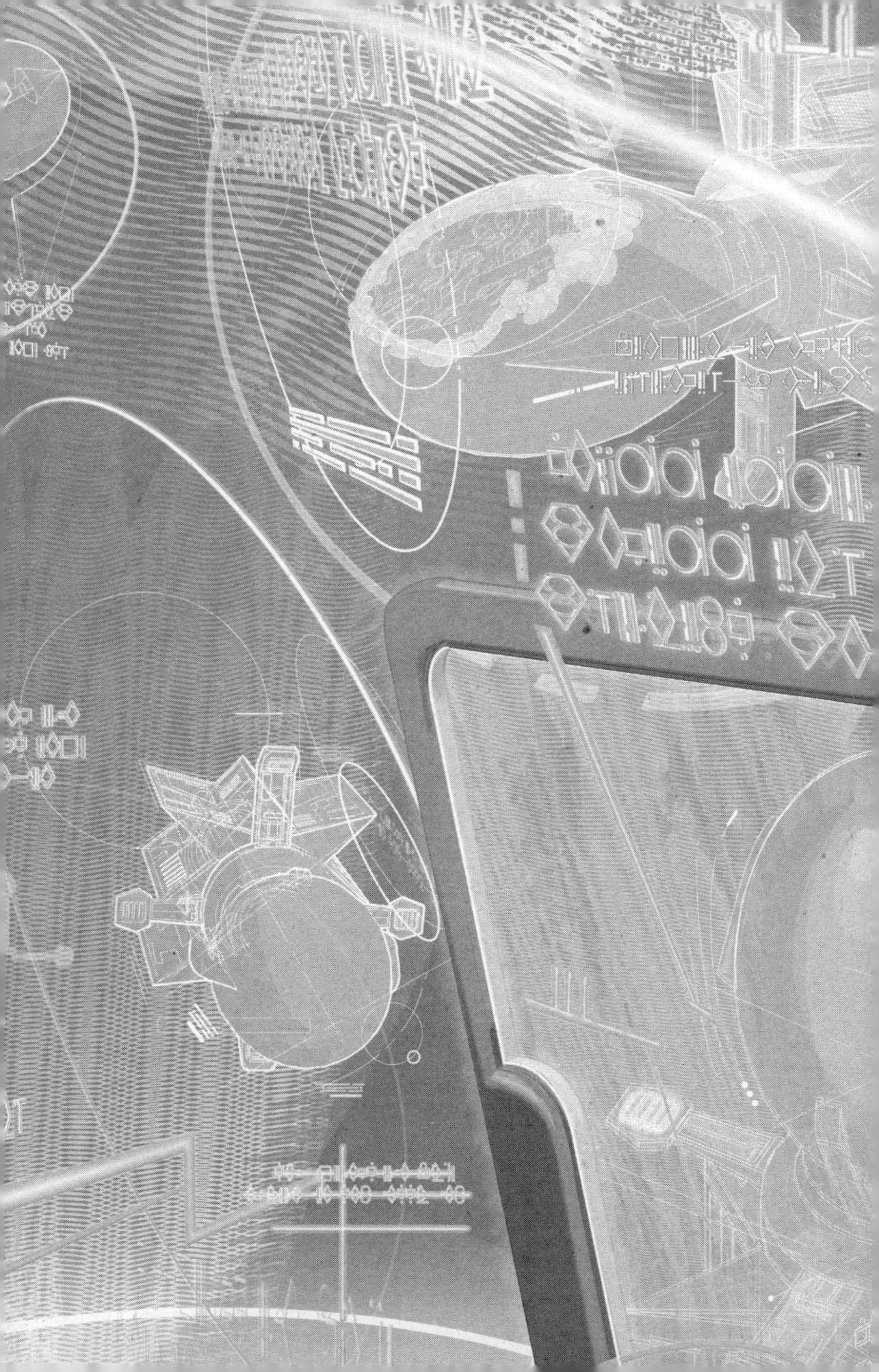

device looked just like the rockets Clark had read about in science-fiction books. Metal that looked like shining skin and clusters of sensors that resembled eyeballs seemed to say that this wasn't a craft that had been built on Earth.

Clark reached out and touched the smooth surface of the rocket. The ship hummed as if waking up from a deep sleep. A beam of light flashed across the barn's interior as an unfamiliar landscape shimmered to life in midair.

"Hello, Kal-El," said a deep voice. "I am Jor-El. I am your father. This is Lara. This is your mother. You were not born on Earth, Kal-El. You were born on the planet Krypton, a world of great scientific achievement and adventure."

Clark watched, speechless, as the faces of a man and a woman appeared in the air. Jor-El's voice continued, revealing more sights of the alien world called Krypton—*his* world, Clark now understood. If Krypton was where he had been born, then it

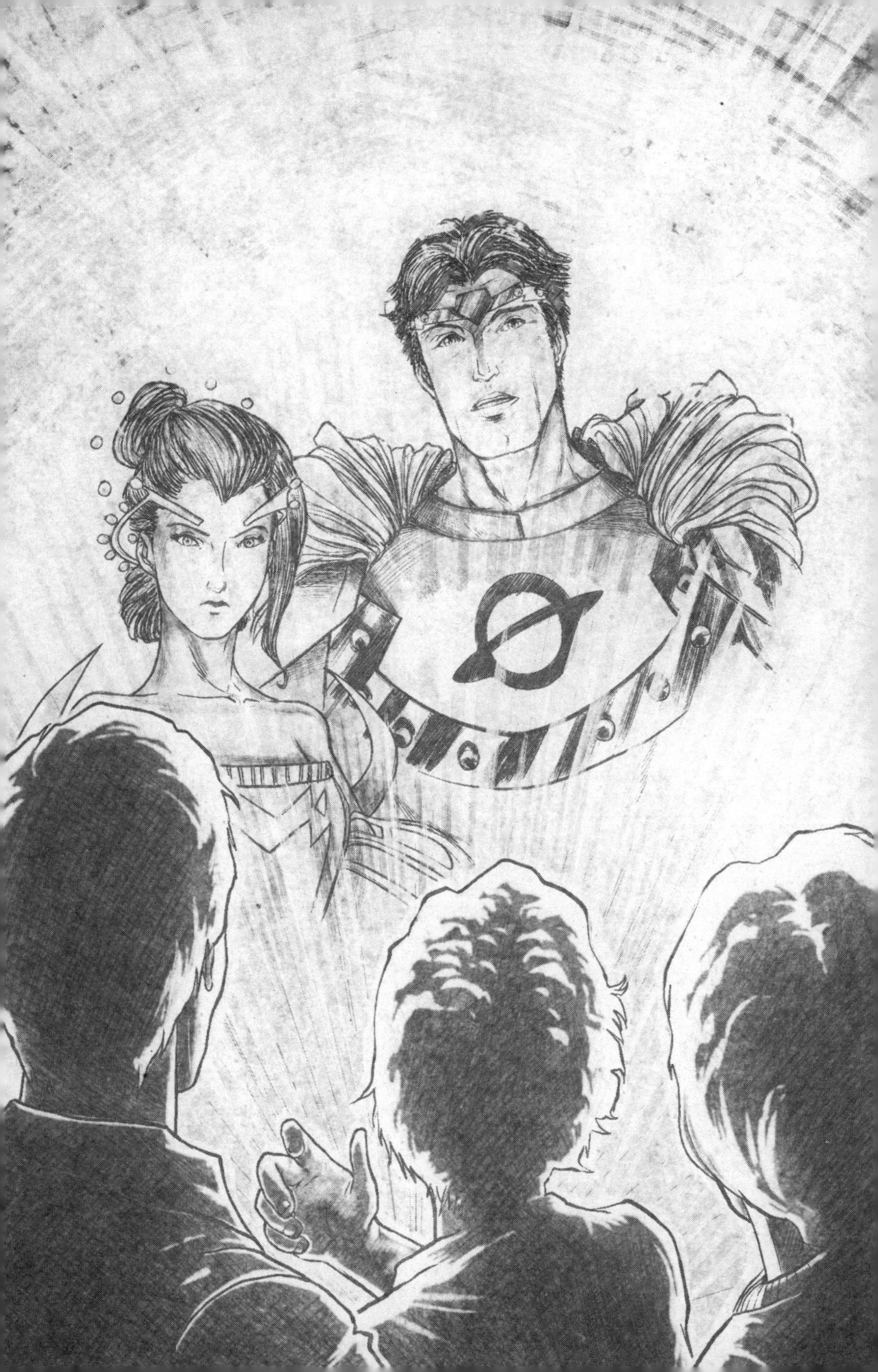

Krypton and the Kryptonians

The Kryptonians were more advanced in the fields of engineering and science, compared to civilization on the planet Earth. The people of Krypton looked almost identical to human beings on Earth, but Krypton had a red-colored sun that gave off a special type of radiation. These red rays prevented the Kryptonians from developing their natural superpowers. When exposed to a yellow sun like the one at the center of Earth's solar system, the cells in a Kryptonian's body are supercharged by the solar energy and allow for amazing feats of strength, speed, and toughness.

should have been his home. But why had he been sent away?

Jor-El recited the names of the great cities of Krypton as the hologram displayed new wonders. Some cities seemed to be made from sharp-edged crystals. Others had rounded corners like polished stones, or ridges like coral reefs that Clark recognized from his biology textbooks. Under a red sun, glittering airships carried passengers from building to building.

Some Kryptonians carried strange weapons in their arms and seemed to be soldiers, while others studied rows of strange symbols projected on the surfaces of intricate machines. These were members of Krypton's scientific and military guilds, explained

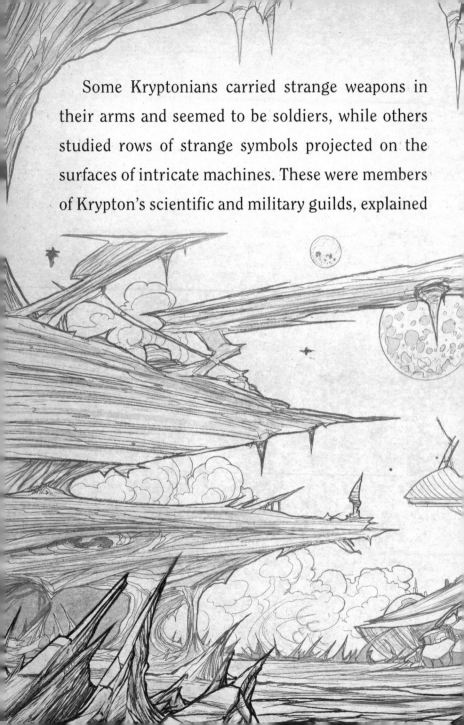

Jor-El, as the hologram zoomed to a new spot on Krypton. Here, in the barren desert, a crack split the surface. An unhealthy green glow shone from inside. As Clark watched, a quake shook the ground and widened the crack even more.

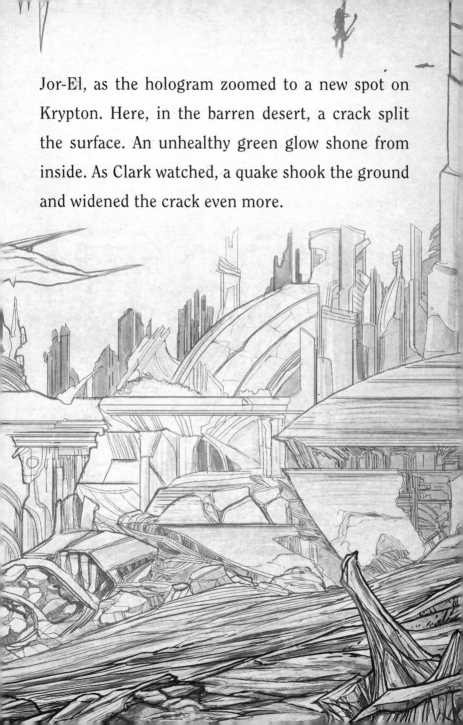

This, Jor-El explained, had doomed Krypton. Something had gone wrong deep in the planet's core. Poisonous radiation had led to severe disturbances, which soon grew so strong they threatened to tear Krypton to pieces.

Krypton's Ruling Council didn't believe Jor-El's warnings and didn't do anything to stop it. There weren't enough space vehicles on Krypton to evacuate the population.

Jor-El knew that he and Lara could not escape. But a small rocket, large enough to carry a baby, could possibly provide a new life for their infant son, Kal-El.

Clark saw images of a baby boy—of *himself*—lying inside the rocket as it sealed itself shut and blasted into space. The next view, taken from the rocket as it sped away to safety, showed Krypton as it exploded in a flash of fire.

At last, Clark understood why the blades of a thresher couldn't cut his skin, or why he could see

AS A BABY, KAL-EL SOARED INTO SPACE JUST AS KRYPTON EXPLODED.

Jor-El and Lara

Jor-El was one of Krypton's top scientists. He discovered the existence of a separate dimension, the Phantom Zone, where criminals could live out their sentences as ghostlike beings. He also learned that his home-world was tearing itself apart and would soon explode. Jor-El's wife, Lara, a graduate of Krypton's Military Academy, was the only other person who believed his warnings that their planet did not have long to live. Knowing that their evacuation rocket was not big enough for the two of them, Jor-El and Lara chose to send their baby, Kal-El, into the safety of space.

bones as easily as the X-ray machine at the Smallville hospital. He was a Kryptonian, and he gained his powers from the rays of Earth's yellow sun.

"You will be free to move among the people of Earth," said Jor-El. "But never forget, although you look like one of them, you are *not* one of them."

That last sentence was not what Clark wanted to hear. Still stunned by everything he had just learned, he ran out of the barn and into the familiar quiet of the cornfield.

It was there that his father found Clark, shivering and alone.

"I don't want to be different," said Clark, tears in his eyes. "I want to be your son."

Jonathan Kent pulled his boy in for a warm hug. "Clark, you *are* my son," he promised.

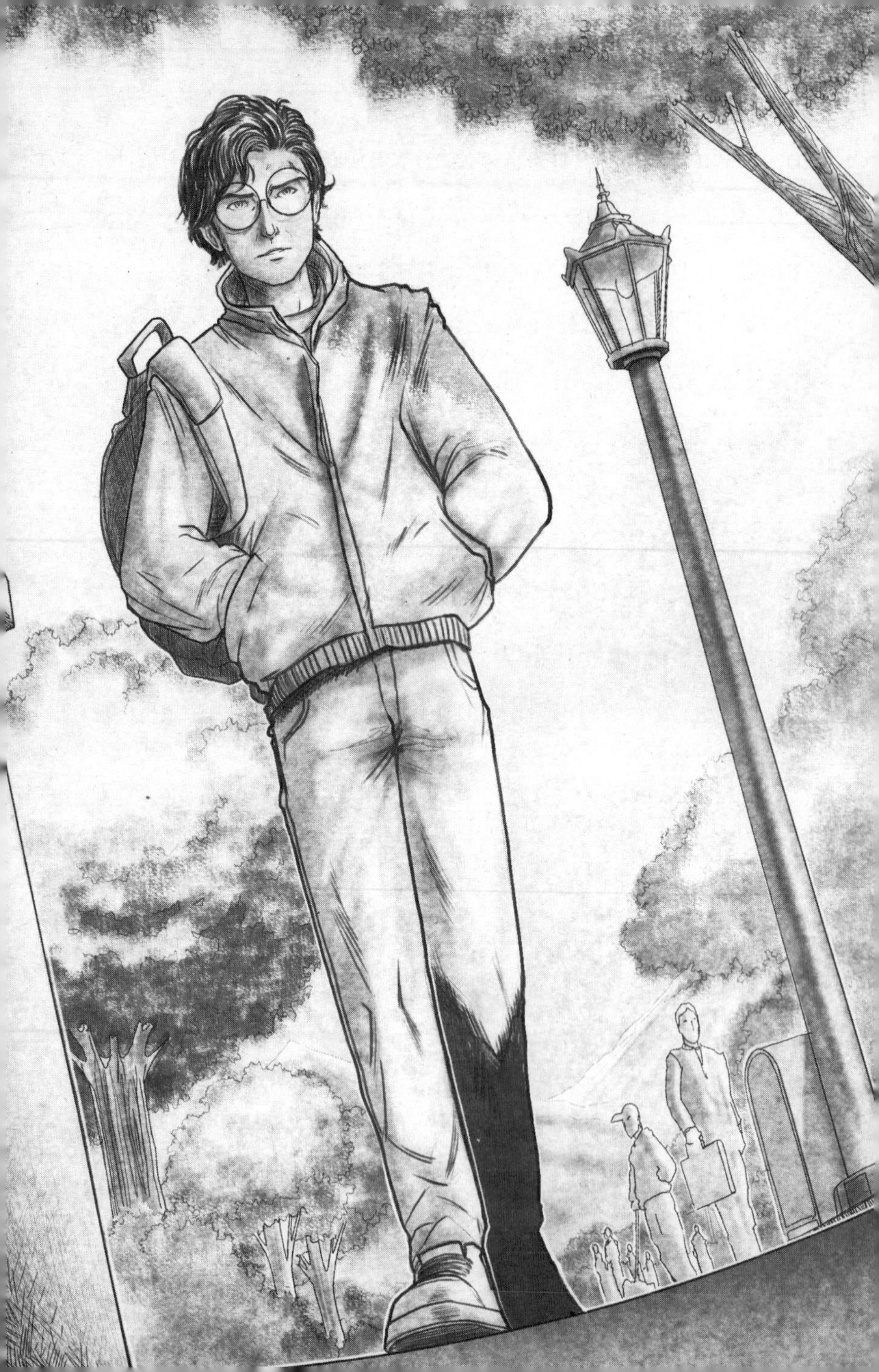

CHAPTER THREE

LEARNING TO BE A HERO

From then on, things changed for Clark. Having answers to the biggest mysteries in his life turned out to be a huge relief.

Clark now knew that his powers weren't some freakish mistake, but were actually a natural gift. He also knew that his birth parents had loved him. And he was grateful that he had been lucky enough to find adoptive parents who loved him just as much.

His new confidence came with an element of caution. Clark needed to be extra careful to keep his extraterrestrial history a secret from others. After all, there was no way of knowing how people would react to news of an alien at Smallville High School!

It wouldn't help if he kept having accidents, like the heat vision mishap that had set a fire in the school hallway. Using a clear, glass-like material found in the rocket, Clark's parents made a pair of glasses that blocked Clark's heat vision before it could fire. Clark also stopped hanging out with his classmates like he used to, worried that he might hurt someone again. Lana, who already knew his secret, was the only person he felt comfortable with.

Before too long, Clark met a new arrival in Smallville: a boy his age named Lex Luthor. The Luthor family wasn't well-liked among the other residents of the town, and Lex didn't seem interested in making friends. He thought he was smarter than everyone else, and Clark found it hard to argue. By all measures, Lex was a genius.

Lex only seemed to care about two things: outer

space and Metropolis. His interest in space led him to collect meteorites that had fallen to Earth, including glowing green rocks that made Clark feel sick whenever he got too close. And every chance he got, Lex bragged about his plans to leave Smallville

CLARK FELT A CONNECTION TO LEX, BUT LEX WOULDN'T EVEN TALK TO HIM.

and make a name for himself in Metropolis. There, he promised, he would build incredible things and discover all-new branches of science.

Clark had been spending more and more time by himself, and in Lex Luthor he recognized someone else who didn't quite fit in. But all his efforts to become Lex's friend were rejected—Lex didn't seem interested in anyone who wasn't a genius like himself. Clark didn't stop trying, however. He felt that there were big futures waiting for both of them.

The changing of the seasons brought the Smallville County Fair, a big event in a town with simple pleasures. Clark always looked forward to the carnival rides, and he finished his chores early so he could meet up with Lana.

The morning newspaper had warned of a storm. Clark looked around. A gray sky and a choppy wind

Lana Lang

Lana Lang grew up in Smallville where she became one of Clark Kent's closest friends. She learned about Clark's amazing powers at an early age and never told anyone Clark's secret, valuing their bond of trust and afraid of what might happen to Clark if everyone knew the truth. During high school, the two friends developed a romantic affection for each other, but did not go so far as to become boyfriend and girlfriend.

seemed to be the only negatives. Otherwise, it looked like a perfect day.

The tornado came out of nowhere. Growing up in Kansas, Clark had seen funnel-shaped twisters before. He knew to take cover the instant a tornado was spotted. This time, he was right out in the open.

The fairgoers ran for cover. Clark wouldn't join them, not until he was sure that Lana was safe.

At last, Clark caught sight of her. He focused his eyes, zooming in like he did whenever he peered through his father's binoculars. He saw Lana crouched in the grass, using her arms to protect her head from flying debris.

Suddenly, the tornado's winds lifted Lana into the air. Clark didn't think. He only reacted. Running toward the spot where Lana had been moments before, he leapt after her. Clark's powerful legs launched him twenty feet into the air, and then the winds caught hold of him, too.

Fighting to make sense of his surroundings as

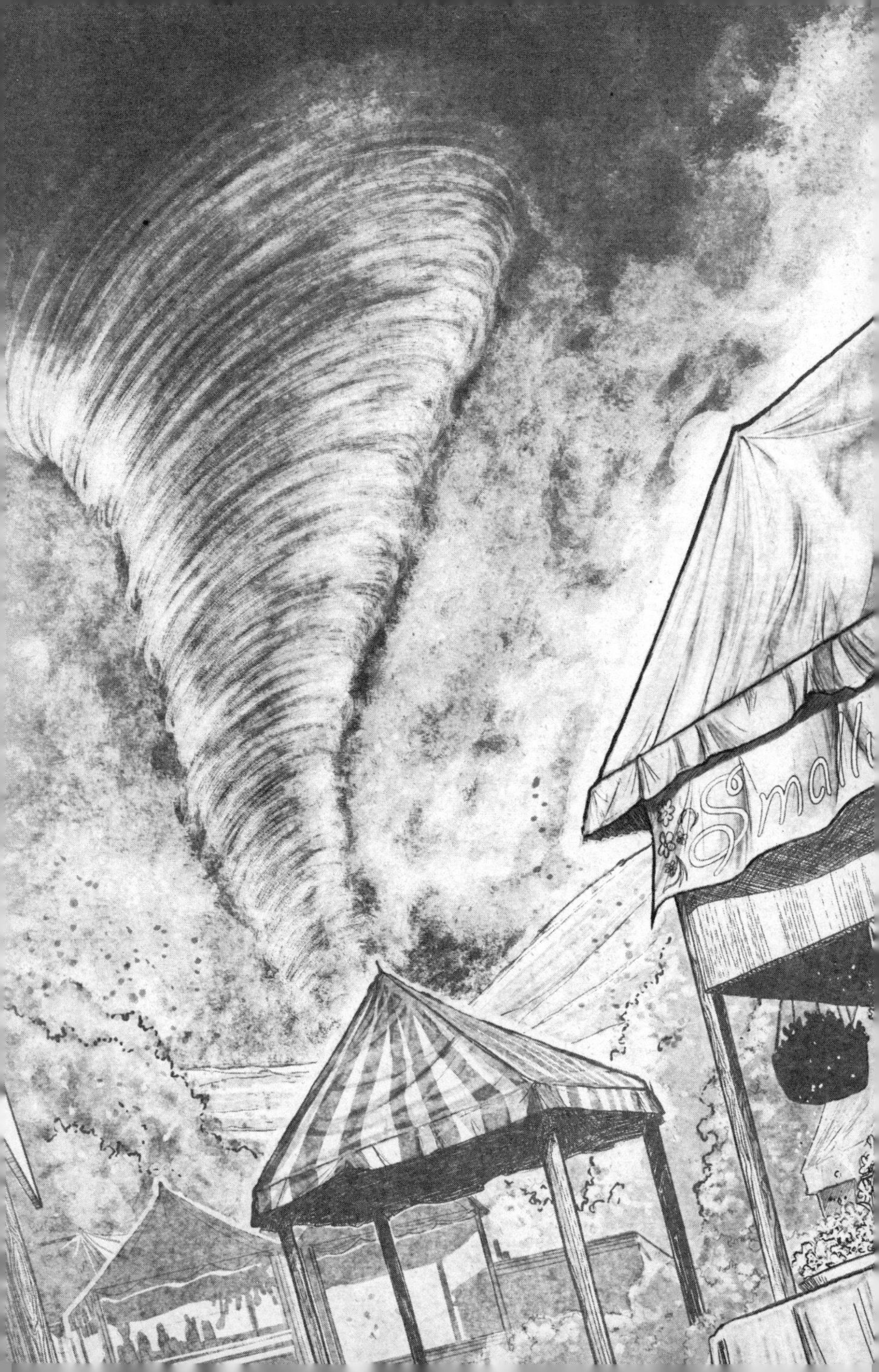

IT TOOK A TORNADO FOR CLARK TO REALIZE THAT HE COULD FLY.

he whirled and tumbled, Clark spotted Lana some distance away. He stretched his arms toward her, and as he did he somehow closed the distance between them. Clark grabbed Lana in a tight hug. It was like the wind had obeyed his commands!

The winds passed around them, and the tornado headed to the north—safely away from Smallville. As he watched the funnel grow smaller, Clark realized that he and Lana were still hanging in the sky.

Clark looked down at his sneakers. He saw the grass far below. Lana gasped as she realized what was happening.

Clark shouted in surprise, plunging halfway to the ground before he came to his senses and stopped his fall. Holding Lana tightly, he dove and whooshed over the fields—inches above the top of the grain stalks.

He could fly!

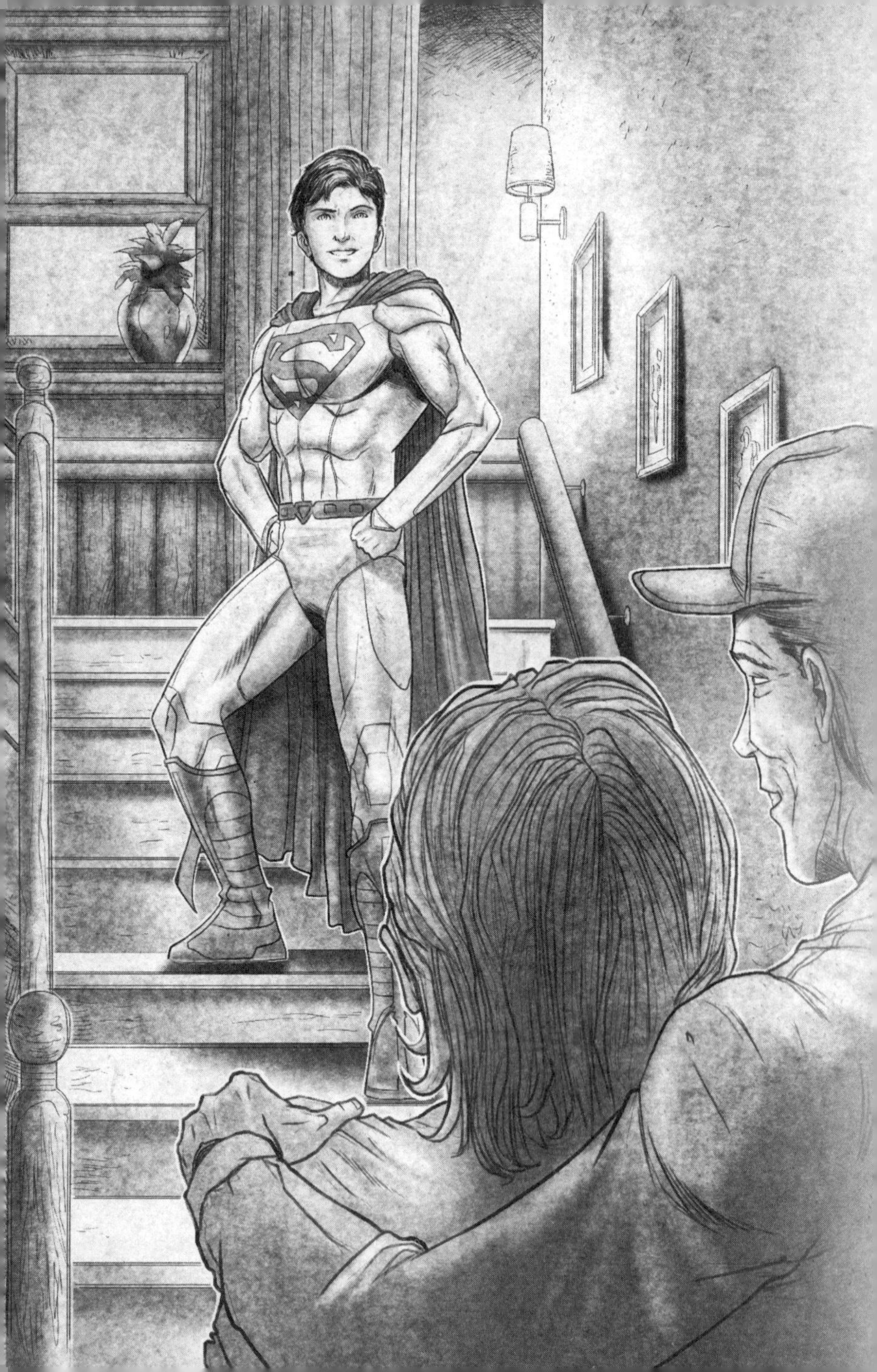

CHAPTER FOUR

STRANGE VISITORS

The discovery that he had the power of flight was the final piece Clark needed. He knew how he wanted to use his amazing gifts.

With his abilities, he could travel into danger without getting hurt. He could move at speeds that guaranteed no one would recognize him. He could soar high above Smallville, scanning for trouble with his incredibly sharp eyes.

Clark told his parents about his plans, ready for them to say no. To his surprise, they agreed. Not only that, his mother announced that she had a surprise for him.

Martha Kent had been visiting the rocket stored in the barn, watching hologram replays of life on Krypton. She had noticed the clothing the Kryptonians had worn, and in the rocket she had found a blanket that Jor-El and Lara had used to keep their baby warm during his long journey to Earth.

Martha showed Clark his surprise—a new costume!—explaining that it looked similar to the ones she had seen the Kryptonians wearing in the recordings from his home-world. It was a tight-fitting outfit in red, blue, and yellow, with a long cape hanging down in back. The triangle-shaped symbol on the chest, which looked like the letter *S*, was actually the family crest of Clark's Kryptonian ancestors in the House of El. Martha smiled as she showed off the outfit, hoping that her son would be proud of this reminder of his birth parents and their history.

CLARK'S KRYPTONIAN BABY BLANKET.

Clark felt a little embarrassed when he put on the outfit for the first time, like a kid whose mother had picked out his Halloween costume. But as soon as he flew into the sky, he could feel the wind rushing smoothly past his streamlined body. Listening to the flapping of his cape as he soared under the light

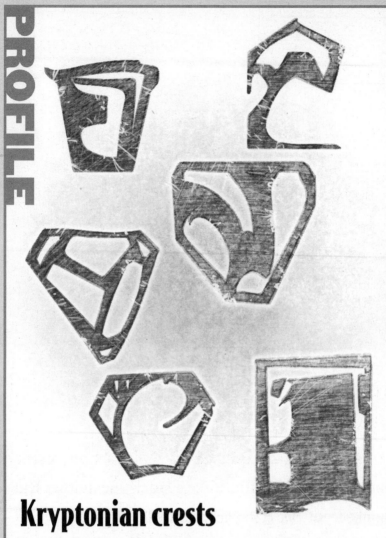

Kryptonian crests

The *S* symbol on Superman's costume doesn't stand for his name. It is the insignia of the House of El, and Superman's father Jor-El wore the same symbol. Other Kryptonians wear different designs, each one of them representing a different family crest.

of a full moon, Clark instantly felt comfortable in his "hero clothes."

Over the next few months, Clark performed good deeds in secret, doing his part to keep Smallville safe. He saved a car from crashing over a hillside. He rescued a family's lost cat from a treetop. He put out a forest fire. The citizens of Smallville soon started swapping stories about a "flying boy," but no one ever suspected Clark Kent.

Clark wanted to keep it that way. But not being able to open up to anyone his age except Lana was frustrating. Clark's extra-sensitive ears heard the other kids as they whispered behind his back, sometimes calling him names.

At the end of one gloomy day at school, Clark loaded his books into his backpack and started the long, lonely walk home. Suddenly, he came face to face with a spectacular surprise.

Three teenagers—two boys and a girl—floated in the air above him. Smiling, they greeted him by name. Each of them wore a colorful costume like his own. They introduced themselves using code names: Cosmic Boy, Saturn Girl, and Lightning Lad.

They were heroes just like Clark, they explained. Not only that, but they were visiting from their normal time line, one thousand years in the future. They had come to say hello to the person who had inspired them to become heroes themselves.

Clark couldn't believe what he was hearing, so the three heroes invited him into their time sphere so he could see for himself. In future Smallville, Clark saw the changes one thousand years had brought.

Gleaming buildings and flying cars weren't nearly as amazing as his new friends. They belonged to an organization called the Legion of Super-Heroes, where each member had a different power. Cosmic Boy controlled magnetism. Lightning Lad used electricity. Saturn Girl could read minds.

Clark met other Legionnaires. All of them wore flight rings giving them the ability to fly, just like

CLARK IS APPROACHED BY COSMIC BOY, SATURN GIRL, AND LIGHTNING LAD.

Clark. Every Legionnaire said the same thing: Their fight for justice wouldn't have happened were it not for Clark's heroic example in the distant past.

His doubts gone, Clark returned to his own time. He shared the details of his adventure with his parents, more convinced than ever that he needed to use his powers to help others.

FUTURE SMALLVILLE IS NOT WHAT CLARK EXPECTS.

PROFILE

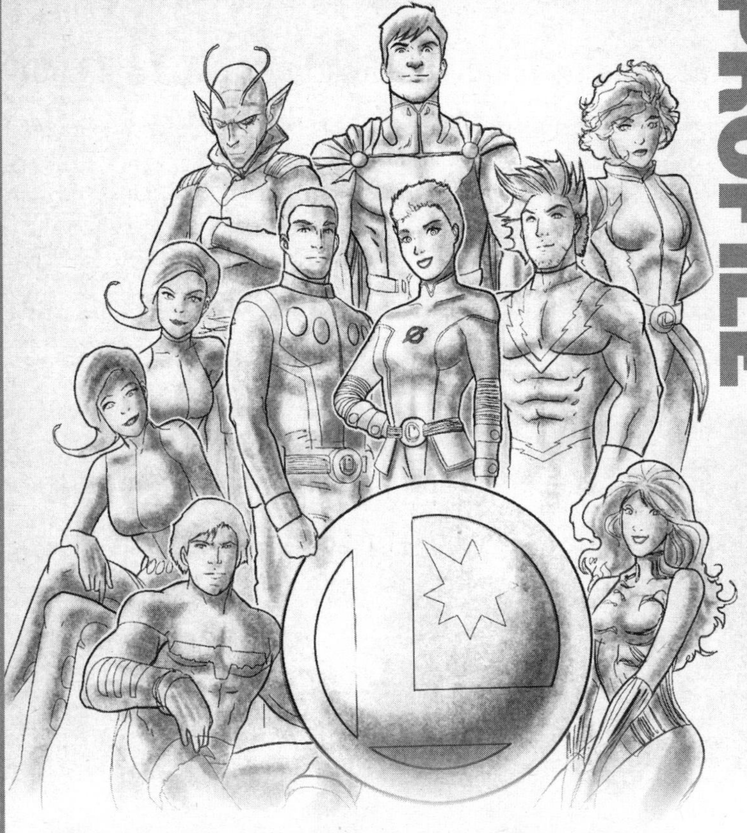

The Legion of Super-Heroes

The Legion of Super-Heroes is made up of superpowered teenage heroes who fight evil in the United Planets a thousand years from the present day. Most of them are aliens from other worlds, and all of them were inspired by the example set by a young Superman. Besides the founding members Cosmic Boy, Lightning Lad, and Saturn Girl, the Legion includes the super-smart Brainiac 5, the shape-shifting Chameleon Boy, the size-changing Shrinking Violet, and the ghost-like Phantom Girl.

At that moment, the roar of an engine split open the sky. Clark rushed outside and saw a rocket streaking overhead. It plowed into the dirt behind the barn.

Clark rushed to the spot, noticing that the spacecraft looked nearly identical to the one that had carried him from Krypton as a baby.

Taking a deep breath, Clark popped open the ship's hatch to see who—or what—was inside.

It was a dog!

Krypto

Because Superman's white-furred dog came from Krypton,
he can store solar radiation in his cells and use it to power
his super-strength, super-speed, flight, and heat vision.
Krypto's senses of hearing and smell are even sharper than
Superman's.

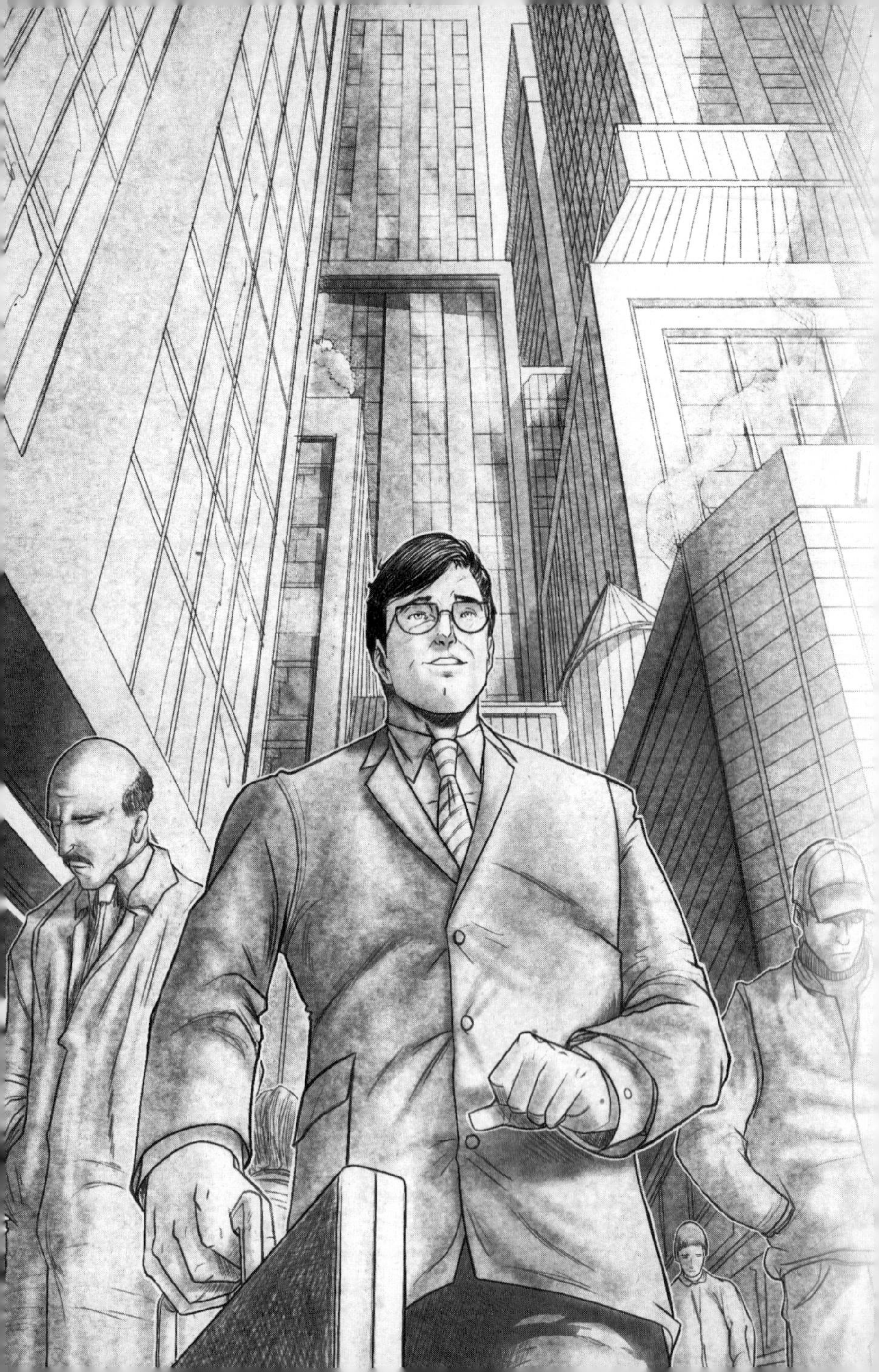

CHAPTER FIVE

MOVING TO METROPOLIS

The Kent family adopted the white-furred animal as their pet. Because the dog had clearly been sent from Krypton before the planet exploded, Clark named him Krypto.

Already, Krypto had many of the same powers as Clark, including incredible strength. Clark knew that Krypto would develop additional powers in time, just like he had.

Time passed, and Clark grew up. After graduating from Smallville High School, Clark went to college

Metropolis

The great city of Metropolis is located on the Atlantic coast of the United States. Its landmarks include LexCorp Tower and the Daily Planet Building. Metropolis is clean and prosperous, but some areas—including the dangerous Suicide Slum—are known for their crime and poverty. Stryker's Island is a maximum-security prison surrounded by water where the city's worst criminals are locked behind bars. Gotham City, home of Batman, is only a short distance from Metropolis.

to study journalism. He had always admired reporters who investigated events and told the public the truth. It was important to Clark that he help people, not just with his superpowers, but also by listening and using his brain.

Clark studied hard and earned his degree. He also took time to travel around the world, meeting people from many different countries. Clark learned that people were essentially the same no matter where they were born or what language they spoke. Most people had good hearts and wanted to do the right thing for their communities.

Clark had a journalism degree, but now he needed a job. For that, he couldn't think of a better place to start than Metropolis. The city had remained in Clark's thoughts ever since Lex Luthor had talked about it back in high school.

Metropolis had many famous newspapers, including the *Daily Planet*, which had fallen on hard times. Clark answered a notice for an entry-level reporter position at the *Daily Planet*, and over the phone he worked out the details with the newspaper's editor in chief, Perry White.

Clark arrived in Metropolis, ready for his first day on the job. He was surprised to see that the city's residents seemed to be in such a hurry. He took his time, admiring the buildings that stretched high overhead, but long-time residents of the city shoved past him and grumbled about the slow-moving stranger on the sidewalk.

Wearing a loose-fitting blue suit and peering through the frames of his glasses, Clark Kent entered the lobby of the Daily Planet Building and pushed the elevator button. The newspaper had definitely seen better days, thought Clark, as he noticed the water-stained paneling and the flickering lights overhead.

Clark stepped out of the elevator as the doors opened on the upper floor. A red-haired boy hurried past him, balancing multiple boxes of donuts in his

THE DAILY PLANET BUILDING IS A FIXTURE OF THE METROPOLIS SKYLINE.

arms. Just as the donut stacks were about to topple, Clark reached out and stopped the fall.

The boy thanked him, introducing himself as Jimmy Olsen. He was the *Daily Planet*'s unpaid intern and spent most of his time running errands, but what he really wanted to be was a photographer. He and Clark exchanged a quick handshake, and

THOUGH THEY RESPECT EACH OTHER, PERRY WHITE AND LOIS LANE OFTEN DISAGREE.

Jimmy headed off. Clark felt better. He had already made a friend!

As Clark approached the door to Perry White's office, he heard loud voices arguing inside. He turned the knob and stuck his head through the door.

Clark recognized Perry White from his photo on the *Daily Planet*'s editorial page. Perry was

speaking with a brown-haired woman who was pointing her finger in his face, making her case that the story she had written deserved to run on the *Daily Planet*'s front page.

Right away, Clark could tell that there was something special about this woman. Courage and stubbornness were qualities often found in people who were champions of the truth. When Clark cleared his throat, both figures turned to face him.

Perry's face widened in a smile. He had been expecting the new arrival. "Lois Lane," he said, "meet Clark Kent."

Lois Lane

Lois Lane is a top investigative reporter for the *Daily Planet*. She is fearless when chasing down a story, and can be extremely stubborn if someone tells her she can't do something. This determination is the reason why she has published so many front-page stories and won a number of journalism awards. Her father is Sam Lane, a general in the US Army, and she has a younger sister named Lucy. Lois grew up on army bases, but she considers Metropolis her home. She admires her fellow reporter Clark Kent for his honesty and fearlessness—two qualities she also admires in Superman!

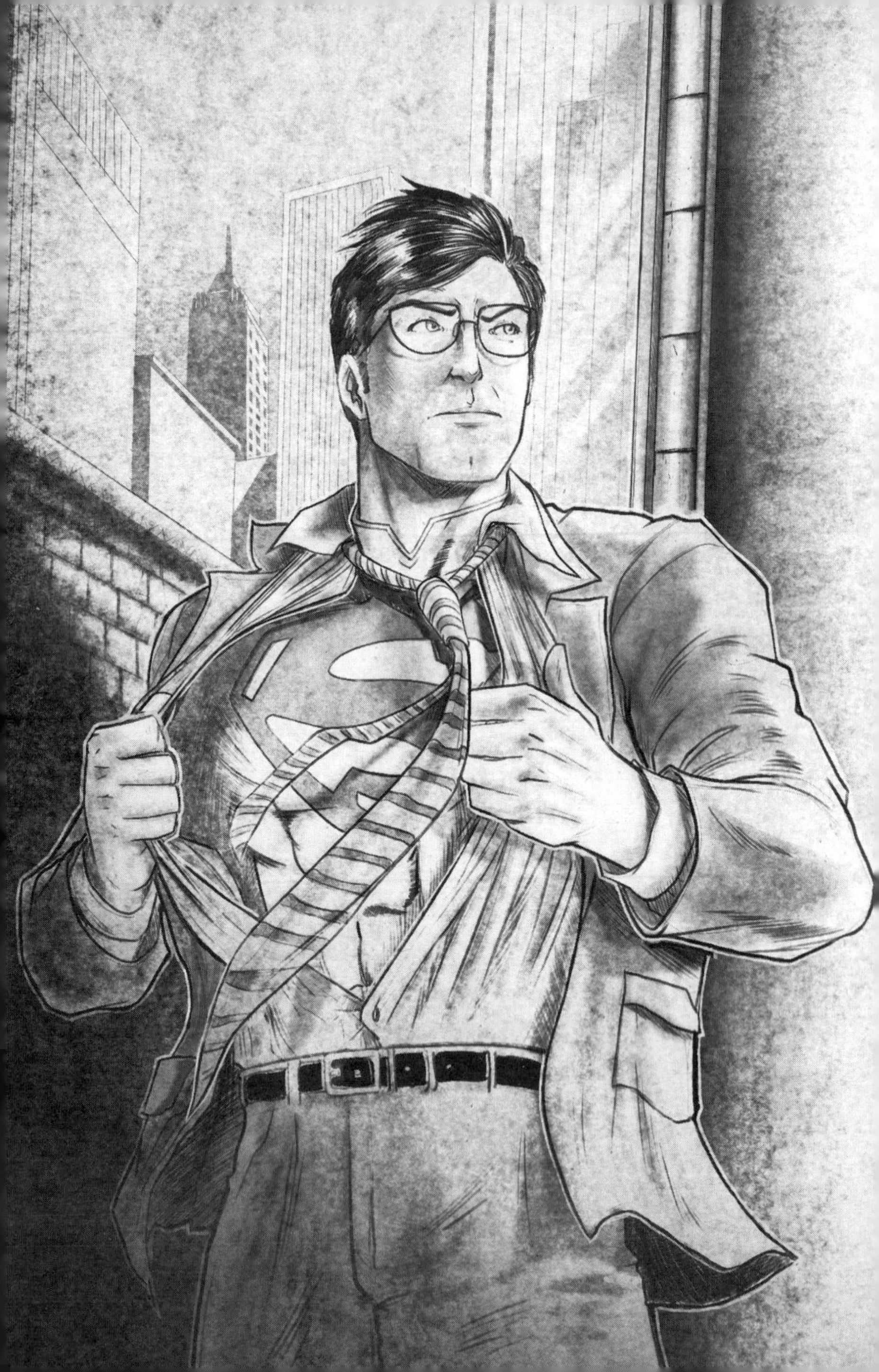

CHAPTER SIX

BECOMING SUPERMAN

Lois shot Clark a hard look. She seemed to pick up everything she needed to know about him in a fraction of a second. Lois didn't seem troubled by the fact that a new reporter might become her rival. Instead, she began thinking about ways she could turn their partnership to her advantage.

Clark followed Lois back to her desk as she shot questions at him. He explained his background in Smallville while Lois gathered up her press badge, a voice recorder, and a blonde wig.

Before Clark knew what was happening, he and Lois had left the Daily Planet Building. They stood across the street from one of Metropolis's newest landmarks: the shining headquarters of LexCorp.

Clark knew that Lex Luthor had made it big in Metropolis after leaving Smallville, but he had no idea *how* big. Lex's scientific inventions had turned him into a billionaire. LexCorp Tower stood as the shining embodiment of Lex Luthor's wealth and power.

Most citizens of Metropolis admired Lex Luthor, but Lois Lane wasn't one of them. Since joining the *Daily Planet*, she had published many stories exposing Lex's illegal business dealings. Today, she planned to go undercover with Clark's help. Lois wanted to find out everything she could about LexCorp's latest project: a mechanical suit made from a special metal alloy, which had been code-named Metallo.

Clark distracted the guard at the building's front gate. Lois put on the blonde wig and scaled the wall. She knew that Lex's security guards would stop her on sight, and she hoped that the disguise would

let her sneak into the press briefing that Lex had arranged for his announcement about Metallo.

Clark couldn't do anything but watch and wait. From his position on the sidewalk, he could see action taking place on the rooftop, where Lex was unveiling his new invention. Suddenly, his sensitive ears picked up the sound of panicked shouting.

Lois had been found out. As security guards closed in on her, the Metallo suit lost its balance and fell over onto its side—knocking a helicopter over toward the edge of the rooftop. As Lois backed away from the commotion, she stumbled and fell straight down the side of the building!

Clark had only seconds to react—but his ability to move at lightning speed gave him a few moments to prepare. Underneath his business suit, he wore the Kryptonian costume his mother had made back in Smallville. Ducking into an empty alleyway, Clark removed his reporter's clothes and raced into action.

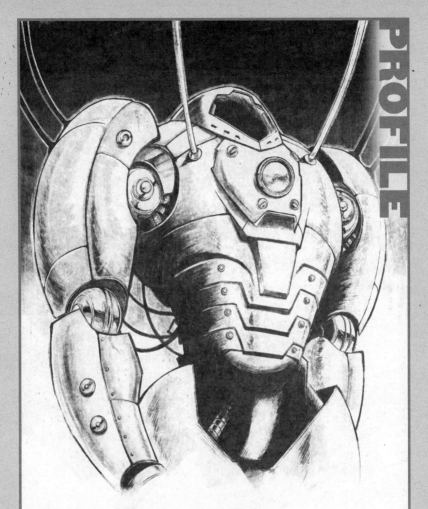

Powered exoskeleton

The Metallo suit developed by Lex Luthor is a type of powered exoskeleton. These machines are worn by single operators. The operator's limb movements are copied by the hydraulic motors of the exoskeleton, providing strength and endurance far beyond human levels.

Still in the middle of her fall, Lois felt a jolt as a strong arm caught her. Her rescuer, hovering many stories above the ground, reached out with his other arm to catch the helicopter as it fell toward them. Lois studied everything she could about the colorful stranger as he set her down on the street.

Clark looked into Lois's eyes. She didn't seem to recognize him as the coworker she had just met a

LOIS DOESN'T RECOGNIZE CLARK.

few hours ago. Already, a crowd had gathered, and as he looked around, Clark knew he could no longer hide his abilities from the public. Not sure how to respond to the crowd's questions, he flew away without answering.

Soaring above Metropolis, Clark spotted Jimmy Olsen sitting on the roof of the Daily Planet Building. In that moment, he knew that both he and Jimmy could use a friend. Though Jimmy didn't recognize Clark, either, the two shared their fears about not fitting in with a city that seemed too big and cold.

Jimmy asked if he could take a photo. Clark agreed. The next day, the *Daily Planet* ran Jimmy's photo on the front page, to accompany a story by Lois Lane. The headline used a nickname given by Jimmy when he noticed that the Kryptonian symbol on Clark's chest looked like the letter *S*.

It read, MEET THE CITY'S NEW SAVIOR—SUPERMAN!

CHAPTER SEVEN

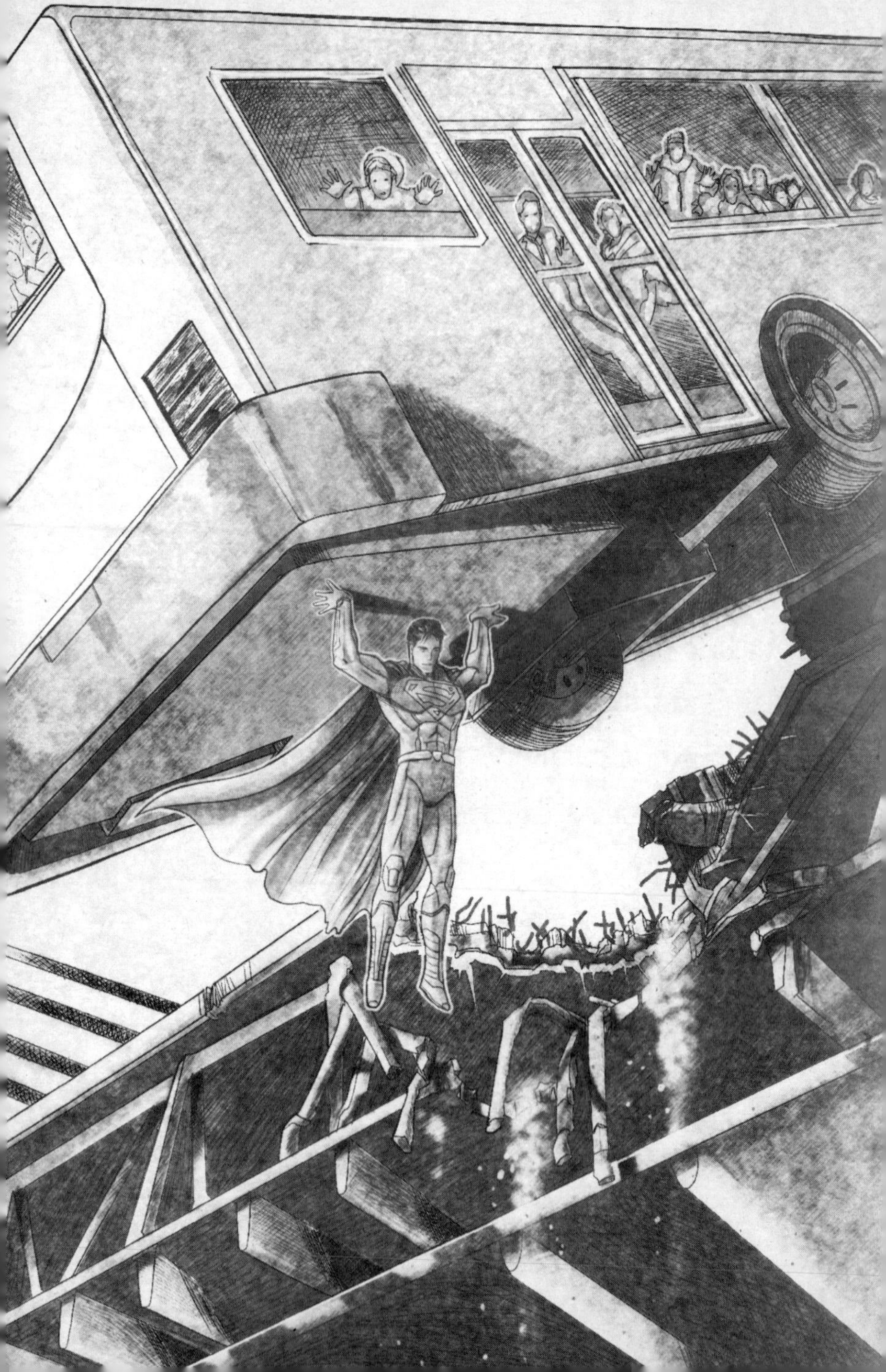

FIGHTING FOR ALL

Every copy of the *Daily Planet* that featured Superman on the front page sold out. No one in Metropolis could stop talking about the amazing powers of this mysterious "Man of Steel." The *Daily Planet* offices got very busy in a hurry, and a grinning Perry White told his reporters to bring him more stories about Superman.

Lois was happy to oblige. For her, Superman was more than just a hot news story. In Superman she saw someone she could trust, and someone who seemed comfortable placing his trust in others. If she could tell Superman's story, it would help everyone realize that they didn't need to be skeptical of this newcomer. For once, the cynical people of Metropolis could find inspiration in a true hero—and maybe they could become better people themselves.

Clark listened to everything that Lois was saying about Superman, but he still couldn't bring himself to tell Lois about his secret identity. The safety of his coworkers—especially those he was growing close to, like Lois—was more important. Clark needed to keep his life as a Super Hero separate from his career as a newspaper reporter, even if he was starting to develop romantic feelings for the smart, brave woman who had thrown him into an adventure in his first day on the job.

Unfortunately, Lex Luthor wasn't going to make things easy. For years, Lex had been the most important person in Metropolis. Now all anyone wanted to talk about was Superman. Jealous and suspicious of the stranger, Lex started his own press campaign.

Lex planted stories with other newspapers, calling Superman an alien and asked the public how they could support a hero who wasn't even human. Clark read the stories. He grew sad when he thought

about the people who wouldn't trust him simply because of where he had been born.

But Lex wasn't satisfied with just negative publicity. His company, LexCorp, worked closely with the military so Lex called in a few favors from a top-ranking general in charge of defending the United States from internal threats. Soon, a squad

LEX IS DETERMINED TO DESTROY SUPERMAN.

of soldiers fanned out across Metropolis, with orders to arrest Superman on the possibility that he might be dangerous.

Sergeant John Corben, a soldier who had volunteered to test LexCorp's experimental exosuit, led the search. Corben had adopted the suit's code name and now answered to the identity of Metallo.

Superman didn't know it, but Lex Luthor had outfitted Metallo with a dangerous surprise. Lex's studies had proven that Superman was weakened by exposure to a certain green meteorite, so Lex used the mineral to provide the power source for Metallo's armor.

When Superman learned that the army wanted to place him under arrest, he didn't know what to do. He wasn't a vigilante who operated outside the law, but at the same time he knew that Lex Luthor had helped plan the operation. If he surrendered, he suspected he might be locked in a prison for the rest of his life.

Superman tried to keep out of the soldiers' reach and avoid hurting them. Soon, however, he found himself cornered in a busy public square. Metallo advanced, using his mechanical strength and the

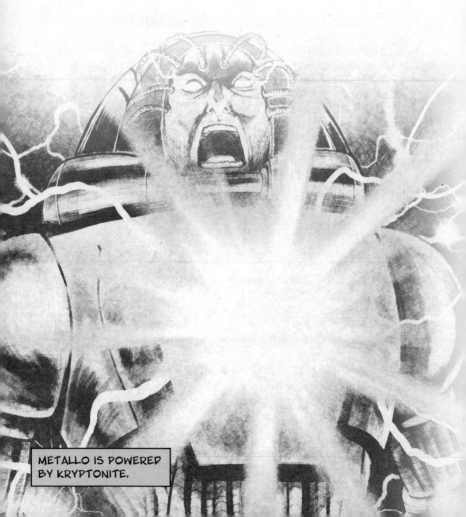

METALLO IS POWERED BY KRYPTONITE.

Kryptonite radiation

The green meteorite rocks from Superman's home-world give off a type of radiation that is harmful to humans and deadly to Kryptonians. Many types of harmful radiation, including gamma radiation and X rays, can be blocked by dense materials including lead.

green, glowing radiation leaking from his chest to bring the Man of Steel down.

Superman didn't want anyone to get hurt, not even Metallo. Scanning his opponent, he discovered that even if Metallo *looked* like a robot from the outside, John Corben was a man who still needed to breathe. Grabbing onto Metallo, Superman flew straight up to the edge of space, moving fast to minimize his exposure to the Kryptonite. When Metallo passed out from the low oxygen, Superman returned him—safely unconscious—to street level.

It was obvious to everyone that Superman wasn't a danger, no matter how hard Lex Luthor wanted to convince them otherwise. The military called off the hunt for Superman. The people of Metropolis congratulated the Man of Steel on his latest victory.

Later, Superman sat down with Lois Lane for another *Daily Planet* interview. While Jimmy Olsen snapped pictures, Superman gave him a special signal watch. Jimmy was the first friend that he had

SUPERMAN DEFEATS
METALLO USING HIS BRAIN
AS WELL AS HIS BRAWN.

SUPERMAN IS CONGRATULATED.

made in Metropolis. Superman explained that if Jimmy ever found himself in trouble, he only needed to activate the alarm and Superman would be there in an instant.

Lois questioned Superman about his origins. He didn't deny that he was an alien. However, Superman made it clear that no matter where he might have come from, Earth was now his home.

SIGNAL WATCH GIVEN TO JIMMY FROM SUPERMAN.

The *Daily Planet*'s front page announced the news the next morning. The headline read, SUPERMAN IS HERE TO STAY!

WEATHER
Partly cloudy, chance of
showers tomorrow

DAILY

DAILY PLANET

50 CENTS

★★★★ A GREAT METROPOLITAN

SUPERMAN
IS HERE TO STAY!

BY LOIS LANE

At first glance, he should look ridiculous. He dresses in a skin-tight outfit reminiscent of a wrestler from the 1930s, complete with a primary color scheme and a giant "S" on his chest. But it's evident almost immediately that there is nothing ridiculous about this man. Instead, he exudes a quiet confidence through strong features and warm eyes. And that's not an attempt at clever word play. While I'm well aware that he is capable of shooting a sort of heat-ray from his stare, there's no disputing that there's something very welcoming about him. He's the sort of man you'd ask for directions if you were lost. As my mother would say, he has an honest face.

When he sits down with me, I first ask him his name. He smiles, and says he likes the one I already picked out for him. "Superman it is," I say, and we start to talk.

He's noticeably hesitant to speak about his past. He understands that he's become an instant celebrity, but still values his privacy. So to keep it light, I steer the conversation toward the subject of his abilities. "It's all everyone's talking about anyway," I say.

There are the obvious ones that everyone knows by now. He's super-strong and can defy gravity with just a thought. He's also bulletproof, and says he can't remember the last time he's seen a drop of his own blood. As he answers each question, he's completely candid, and remarkably casual about everything, as if he's lived with his phenomenal skill set for quite some time.

And then there are those eyes again. "I have heat vision," he says. "But I can also detect other spectrums of light that most people can't. And I have X-ray vision as well." Needless to say, a bit of an awkward silence follows his last comment before Superman shifts a bit on the couch and then changes the subject. "I also have a sort of super-breath," he says. "It comes in handy for putting out fires. Or…" He stops for second and looks at the glass of water in front of him. Then he blows gently on it, and I watch as the water hardens and freezes before my eyes.

I tell him it's a cute trick, and he flashes his smile again.

"So why the interview?" I ask h "You could have ignored my requ kept to your mystery man routine. trying to set the record straight?"

He gets serious then, and I see side of him I've seen when he's in the field. This isn't a game, and wants that to be apparent. "I've b thinking about it for a while, an think the public deserves to kr something about me. If it was the o way around, I'd want to know what going on. How a man can do all th things. And… I may not be up explaining everything just yet, or e know how to, really, but I just wan people to know. I want them to rea they don't have to be afraid of me."

He stands up then, and places glass of ice on the table.

"Thanks for the drink, Miss Lar he says, as if the simple gesture o cold beverage means the world to h

I smile as he heads over to balcony and opens the door. Th I watch a man in a silly red cape into the air and look nothing shor majestic. It's not until he's gone t I realize that I believe every word told me.

LOIS'S ARTICLE SOLIDIFIES SUPERMAN'S SUPER HERO STATUS.

Photograph by James Olsen

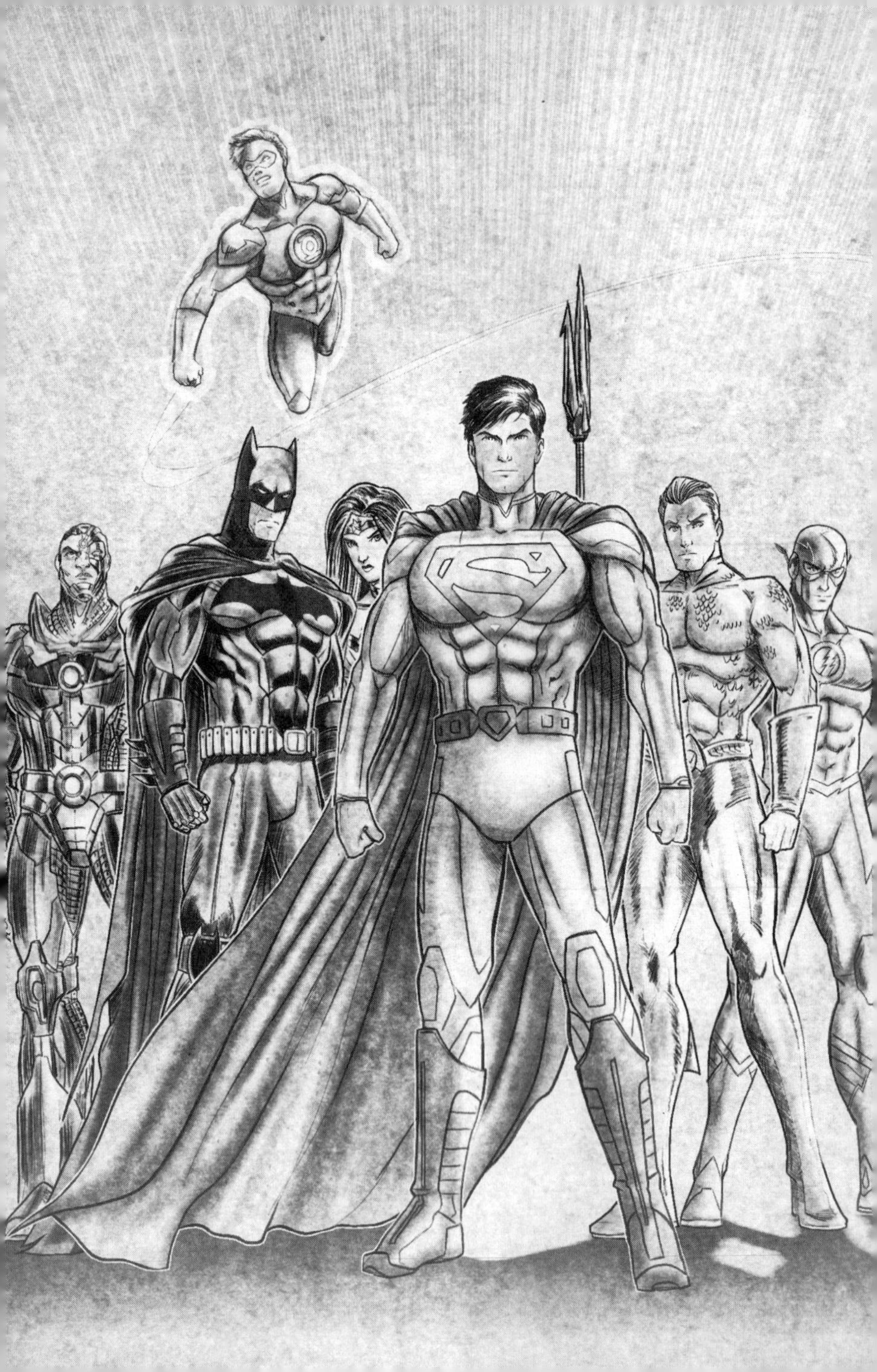

CHAPTER EIGHT

AMAZING ALLIES

Superman's success in Metropolis was the first time that a Super Hero had made an impact in the lives of ordinary people. With the Man of Steel setting an example for others to follow, heroes started showing up in every corner of the globe.

In Central City, a man who could run faster than the speed of sound began fighting crime as The Flash. From the mysterious island of Themyscira, Diana of the Amazons announced her crusade against evil as Wonder Woman. In Detroit, a top

95

athlete was rebuilt with machine parts to become Cyborg. From the ocean realm of Atlantis, a water-breathing king came to the surface-world as Aquaman. From Coast City came Green Lantern, who belonged to a corps of intergalactic peace-keepers.

Superman kept his eye on the new arrivals and made an effort to welcome each of them as fellow champions. It was in nearby Gotham City that he crossed paths with Batman, meeting one of the most interesting new heroes. Batman didn't have any special abilities, but he did have the brilliant mind of a detective as well as many gadgets that allowed him to scale buildings and knock enemies unconscious. Superman, who was open and friendly, didn't seem to have much in common with the secretive and mysterious Batman. But they shared the goal of keeping the world safe, and soon the two became close friends.

Batman's young partner, Robin, looked up to Superman. He even asked for an autograph.

UNLIKELY FRIENDS, SUPERMAN AND BATMAN BOND IN THEIR QUEST FOR JUSTICE.

The Justice League

The Justice League has included many different heroes throughout its history. Other members have included Hawkgirl, Green Arrow, Black Canary, the Martian Manhunter, and the Atom. At different times the Justice League's headquarters has been located in a satellite orbiting the Earth and even on the surface of the moon.

Superman answered the request by using his heat vision  to etch his name into a steel beam.

After meeting a few of the new heroes, Superman realized that some challenges might be bigger than he could handle on his own. He convinced the others to team up if Earth ever faced a grave danger. These seven heroes—Superman, Batman, Aquaman, Cyborg, Green Lantern, Wonder Woman, and The Flash—became the Justice League.

Superman's responsibilities to the Justice League left less time for him to handle problems around Metropolis, not to mention the time he needed to work in his job as *Daily Planet* reporter Clark Kent. Superman didn't want to spend all his hours as a Super Hero. Fortunately, the people of Metropolis were ready to answer the challenge.

The Metropolis Police Department formed a new division, the Special Crimes Unit. The goal of the SCU was to handle robots, monsters, mutants, and other dangers that fell outside of normal police work. Superman worked closely with the SCU and its leader, Captain Maggie Sawyer.

Elsewhere in Metropolis, many top scientists lent their brainpower to S.T.A.R. (Scientific and Technological Advanced Research) Labs. Superman,

CAPTAIN MAGGIE SAWYER AND THE SCU ARE ALWAYS PREPARED.

The city of tomorrow

One of the unique qualities of Metropolis is that the city encourages the development of advanced technology and experimental inventions. S.T.A.R. (Scientific and Technological Advanced Research) Labs is one of the most futuristic research facilities in the world and is responsible for investigating extraterrestrial technology and new forms of energy in the hope that the discoveries will benefit everyone on the planet. Superman is friends with many scientists at S.T.A.R. and often asks them for advice.

who knew that brainpower was often more important than super-strength, made friends with Professor Emil Hamilton at S.T.A.R. Labs. He soon learned that there was no one better at investigating strange energy surges or figuring out how to operate weird alien devices.

Best of all, Superman soon faced the surprise arrival of another Kryptonian like himself! Kara Zor-El had escaped the destruction of Krypton in a similar rocket, but she arrived on Earth years later during the height of Superman's fame. Kara was Superman's cousin, and knew a great deal about Kryptonian culture.

Earth's yellow sun gave Kara the same powers as Superman, including flight, strength, speed, and bulletproof skin. She designed a similar costume, and soon joined her cousin's fight as Supergirl.

Superman now had a living connection to the past he thought he'd lost forever. Supergirl shared her knowledge of their vanished culture, while

PROFESSOR EMIL HAMILTON WAS AN IMPORTANT ALLY TO SUPERMAN.

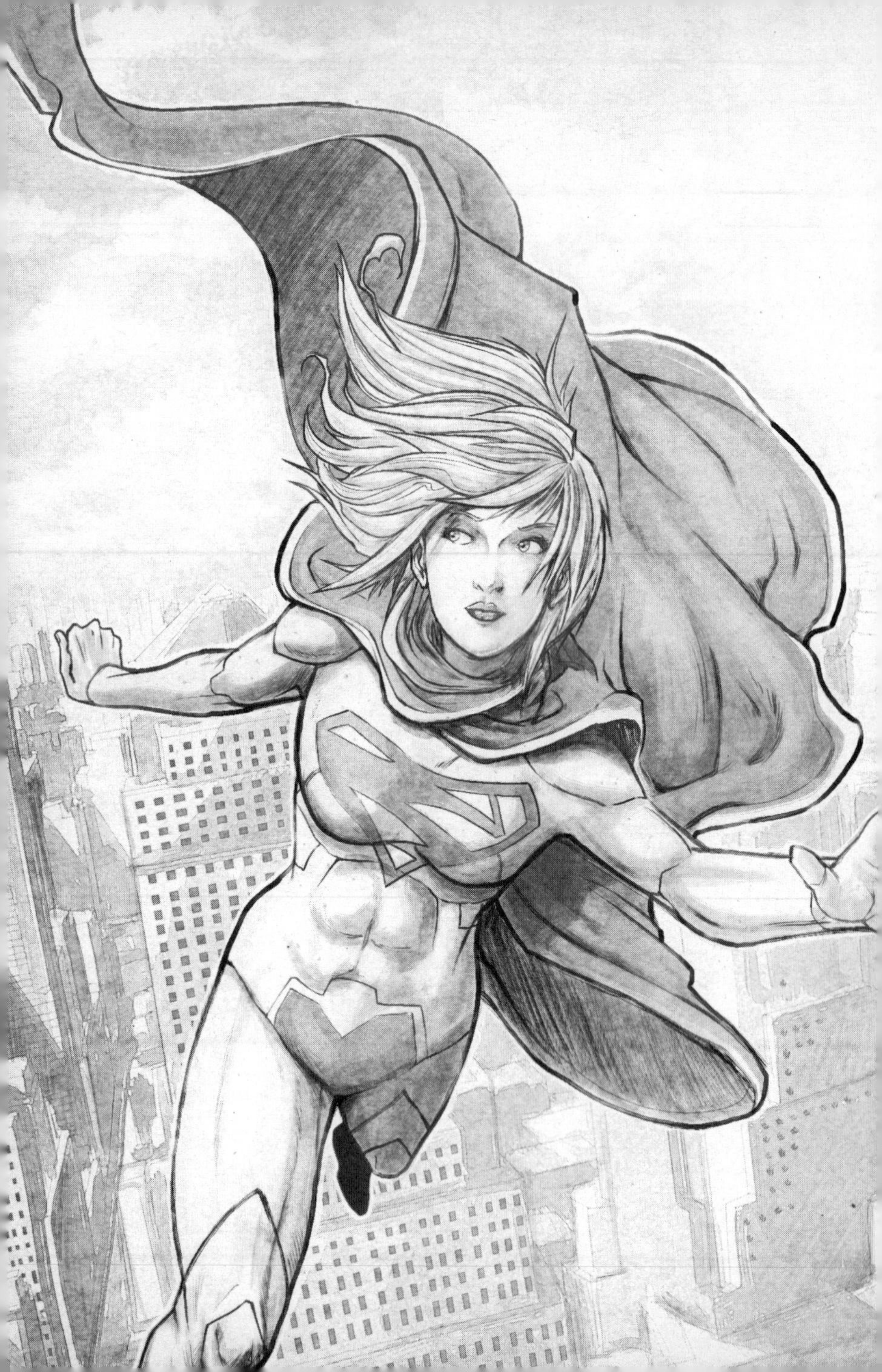

Superman helped his cousin get used to life on Earth. The planet now had three protectors from the world of Krypton!

ON EARTH, SUPERGIRL LEARNS TO USE HER SUPERPOWERS, TOO.

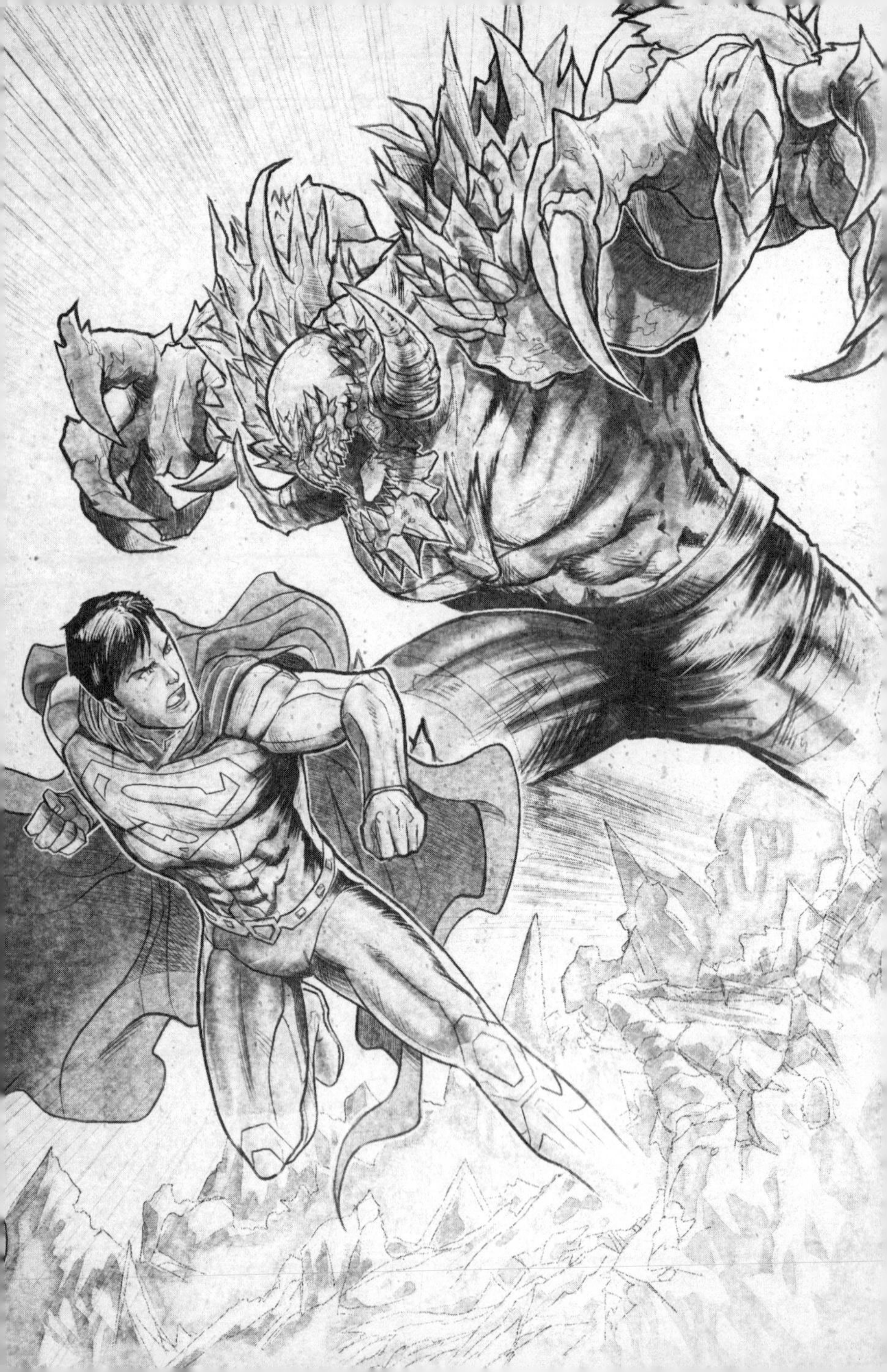

CHAPTER NINE

FEARSOME FOES

Superman and Supergirl weren't the only Kryptonians to have survived the destruction of their home-world. Unfortunately, though, the others were some of Krypton's worst criminals!

For centuries, the Ruling Council of Krypton had sentenced guilty offenders to imprisonment inside the Phantom Zone—a dimension where they would live like ghosts, unable to return to the real world. Existing in this way meant that the Phantom Zone criminals, like Doomsday, all survived the explosion of Krypton. Eventually, the worst convict of them all discovered how to escape.

His name was General Zod, and the Council had banished him to the Phantom Zone for trying to overthrow the planet's leaders and make himself the ultimate ruler of Krypton. Zod didn't care about anyone. He only wanted power, and he hated the weak.

When General Zod broke out of the Phantom Zone, he brought his two closest lieutenants. Seeing the destruction caused by the three villains across the cities of the globe, Superman realized just how dangerous Kryptonians could be if they didn't obey their consciences. Zod laughed at the "lesser beings" of Earth, and put their lives in danger while Superman raced to save them. The Man of Steel won the day, but it saddened him to realize that not all Kryptonians were as friendly as Supergirl. Some were violent and warlike, and it was more important than ever that he and Supergirl treat everyone with respect. Superman wanted the people of Earth to welcome their help, not fear their powers.

To gain a better understanding of where he had come from, Superman built a refuge for himself in the frozen wastelands north of the Arctic Circle. Using technology he had found in the rocket that

GENERAL ZOD IS A STRONG LEADER WITH MANY FOLLOWERS.

General Zod

The enemies who fight Superman usually fall into one of two categories: brains or muscle. Villains like Doomsday and Bizarro are mindless fighters, while Brainiac and Lex Luthor are brilliant schemers. But General Zod is both a warrior and a military tactician, and is one of the few enemies who excels on both measures. On Krypton, Zod was the leader of the planet's military. Like Jor-El, he believed the Ruling Council of Krypton was weak and ineffective, but Zod believed that violence was the answer. When Zod tried to take over the government, the Council locked him in a prison dimension called the Phantom Zone. Zod attracted more followers among the criminals of the Phantom Zone until he had created a new army.

brought him to Earth, Superman grew a gigantic structure that towered above the ice.

Inside, Superman found a control board that responded to any question he asked. Here—in what he called his Fortress of Solitude—he began to fill the empty halls with souvenirs from his adventures, such as a steel beam he had twisted into the shape of a pretzel and an experimental space plane he had rescued from a fiery crash.

Krypto, his superpowered pet from Smallville, made his home as the resident watchdog. During his stays at the Fortress, Superman studied his history as a member of the House of El, and searched the databanks for information on new threats.

It couldn't have come at a better time, for Superman soon faced many extraterrestrial foes with ties to Krypton. Brainiac was an ultra-genius from the planet Colu. He had miniaturized the Kryptonian city of Kandor, preserving it in a bottle, which he stored on a shelf inside his spaceship.

THE CITY OF KANDOR WAS BRAINIAC'S PRIZED POSSESSION.

Superman stopped Brainiac when the evil genius tried to do the same thing to Metropolis. The Man of Steel hoped that one day he could save the people of Kandor and restore their city to its full size.

Doomsday was even more dangerous. The creature was an unstoppable warrior, created on Krypton ages ago for no other purpose than to fight and to win. Superman's battle with Doomsday was one of the few times when the Man of Steel lost. Superman battled back, though, and he triumphed in his rematch with Doomsday.

Lex Luthor observed it all, studying the new arrivals to learn from their mistakes. Lex, who still hated Superman, had devoted himself to finding new ways to bring down the hero of Metropolis. Having confirmed that the green meteor rocks were actually fragments from Superman's home-world, Lex used this substance to hurt Superman with Kryptonite rays, Kryptonite darts, and other devices. He even wore a

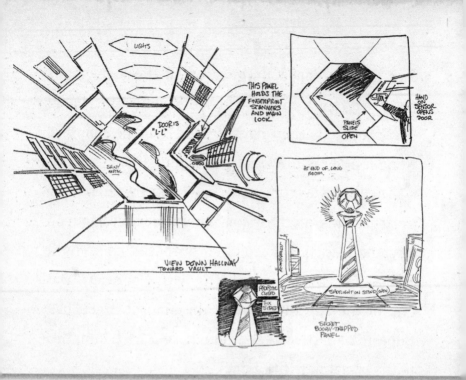

Labels within the image: LIGHTS · DOOR IS "L·L" · SHINY METAL · THIS PANEL HOLDS THE FINGERPRINT SCANNERS AND MAIN LOCK · PANELS SLIDE OPEN · HAND ON SENSOR OPENS DOOR · VIEW DOWN HALLWAY TOWARD VAULT · AT END OF LONG ROOM. · SPOTLIGHT ON STAND (OPEN) · PEDESTAL CLOSED SIX SIDED · SECRET BOOBY-TRAPPED PANEL

DESIGNS FOR LEX LUTHOR'S VAULT TO STORE HIS KRYPTONITE RING.

Kryptonite ring to keep Superman from getting too close. Since Kryptonite radiation could harm humans, too, Lex stored the ring inside a vault if he didn't need it.

Lex hated Superman so much that he wanted to create his *own* Superman—one that would obey his commands without question—in an effort to destroy the Man of Steel once and for all. The laboratories of LexCorp tried. They worked hard to grow a perfect Superman clone, but the procedure failed. What resulted was a superpowered being with blocky features and a malfunctioning brain who often said the exact opposite of what he meant. Salvaging what he could from the botched experiment, Lex named his flawed creation Bizarro.

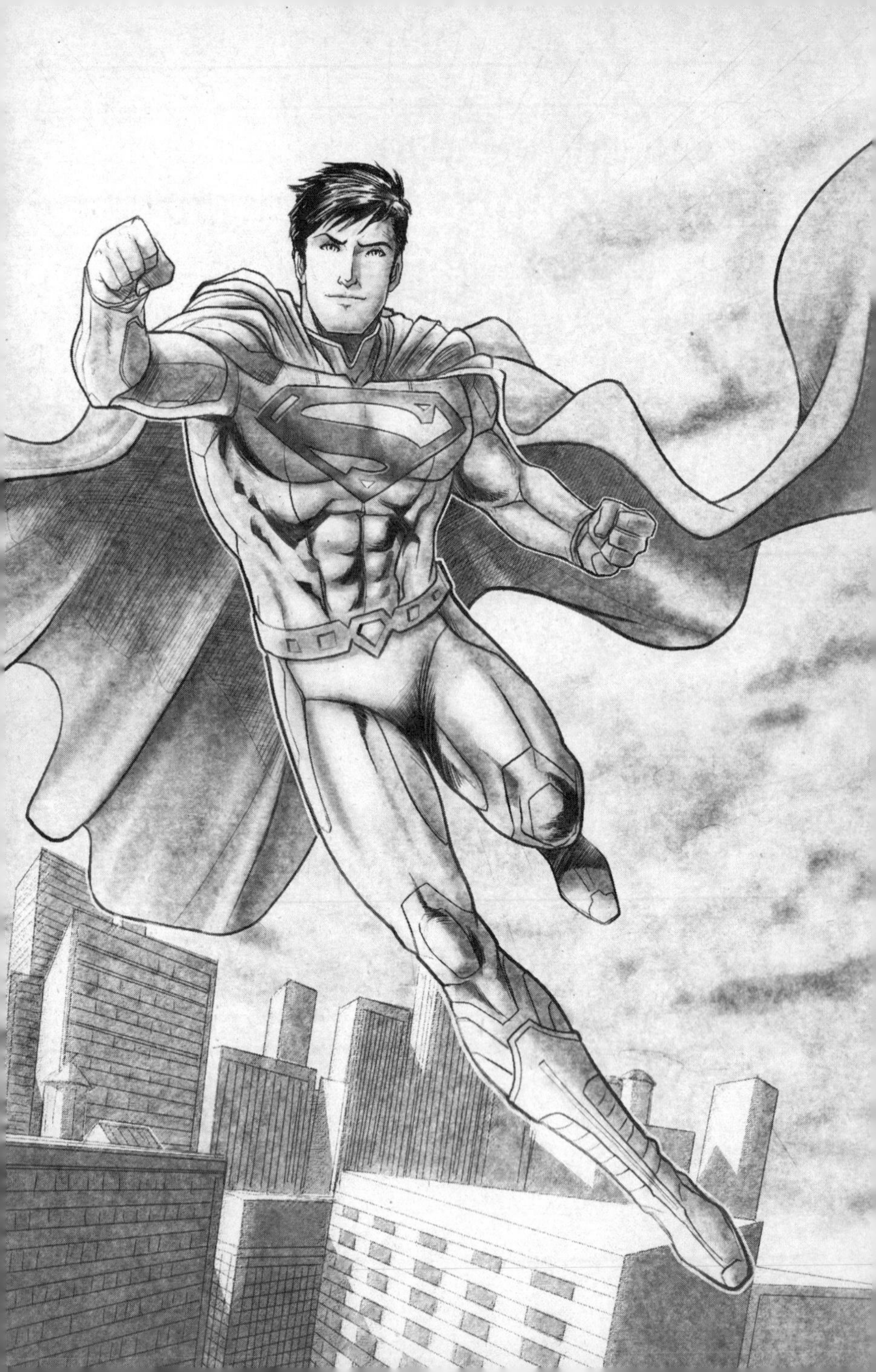

CHAPTER TEN

UP, UP, AND AWAY

I n the years since Superman first rescued Lois Lane in her fall from the roof of LexCorp Tower, the Man of Steel has become one of Metropolis's most important figures. Superman's emergence inspired many technological innovations, from the high-tech weapons of the Metropolis Special Crimes Unit to the futuristic experiments of S.T.A.R. Labs. In response, Metropolis has gained the nickname, "the City of Tomorrow."

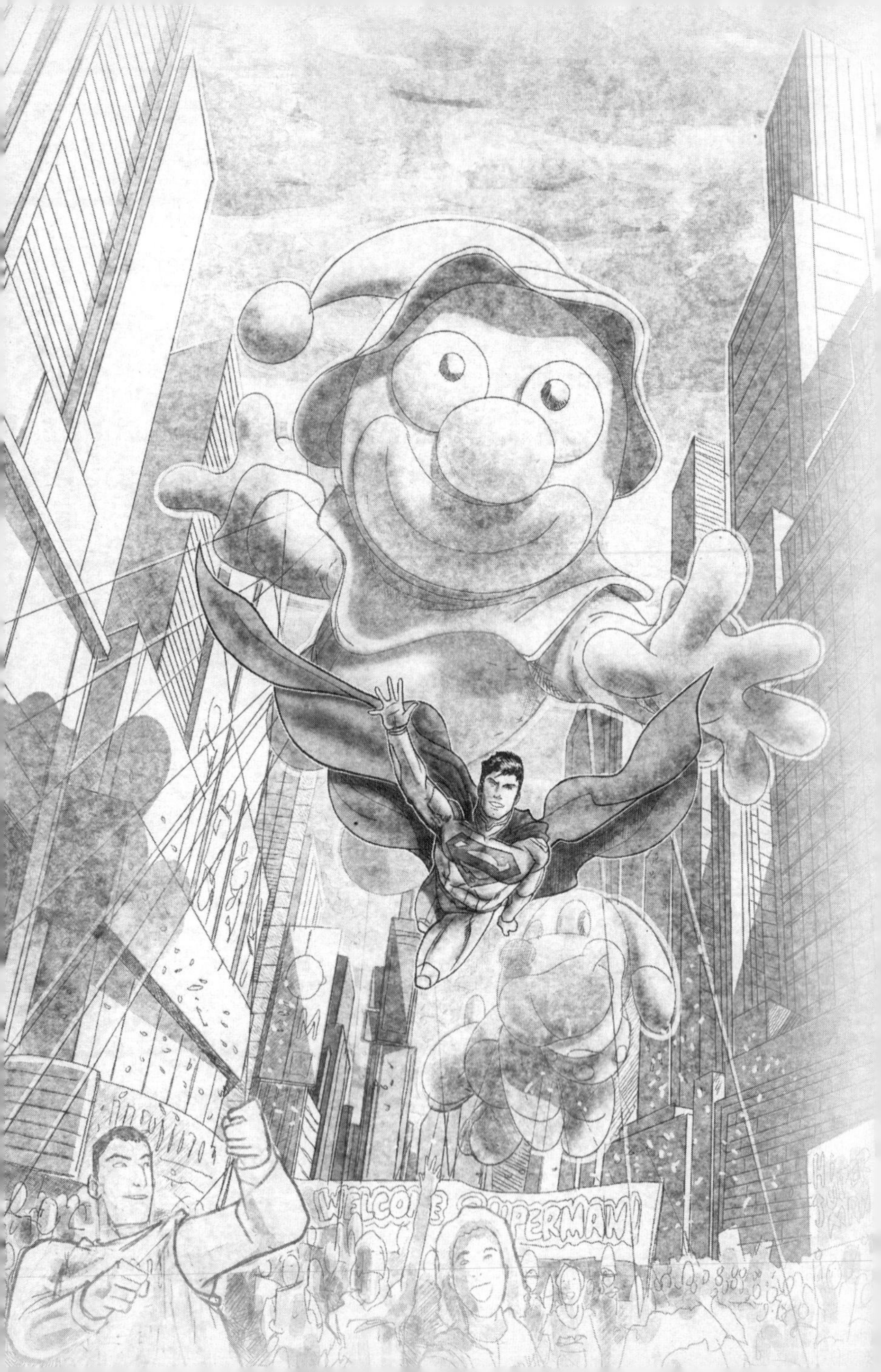
WELCOME SUPERMAN!

Superman has saved the city countless times from villains who wished to destroy it. Metropolis has shown its gratitude. A statue of Superman stands proudly in a public park. Downtown parades frequently feature Superman as the guest of honor. The mayor of Metropolis has awarded Superman the key to the city.

Far more important than public praise is Superman's influence on those who look up to him. Everyone knows that Superman never surrenders, no matter what happens. In this way, people of every age and from every walk of life have found a role model in the Man of Steel. Students, teachers, police officers, firefighters, office workers—every job is important in Superman's eyes, as long as people do their best and help others when they need it.

Most people of Metropolis don't know it, but Superman continues to work as *Daily Planet* reporter Clark Kent. For Clark, it's important to stay grounded. A friend like Jimmy Olsen, or a possible romantic partner like Lois Lane, remind him what he's fighting for every day.

And the fight never ends! Truth and justice are the principles Superman stands for, and no enemy can push him off the path of what's right. Superman

wants everyone to follow that same goal.

"I was given a gift, but all of you were given gifts, too," he said. "Use them to make one another's lives better."

The next time you're in Metropolis, be sure to look up in the sky. Sooner or later you'll see a streak of red and blue. And you'll know—it's Superman!

Fast Facts

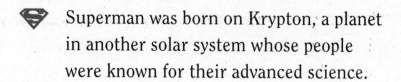 Superman was born on Krypton, a planet in another solar system whose people were known for their advanced science.

Superman's father, Jor-El, discovered the danger facing Krypton, but he could not convince the Ruling Council that the danger was real.

Kryptonians like Superman get their powers from the rays of Earth's yellow sun.

Superman's powers include flight, super-strength, super-speed, incredibly tough skin, X-ray vision, heat vision, and freeze breath.

Lex Luthor believes that *he* should be the savior of humanity, and is jealous that an alien like Superman is more popular than he is.

- Besides wearing glasses, Superman slouches and changes his voice when he appears in public as Clark Kent.

- Because it is made out of Kryptonian material, Superman's costume cannot be ripped or damaged.

- Clark Kent uses his job as a newspaper reporter to learn about problems facing Metropolis, which he can then solve in his role as Superman.

- Superman's enemy General Zod commanded Krypton's military forces, until he tried to overthrow the planet's leaders and ended up in the Phantom Zone.

- Superman can hold his breath for hours, allowing him to swim to the bottom of the ocean or fly into outer space.

- Pieces of the planet Krypton have fallen to Earth as Kryptonite meteorites, which are harmful to Superman.

- Superman's dog, Krypto, has the same powers as Superman, including flight and heat vision.

- The Fortress of Solitude contains an alien zoo, where Superman keeps strange animals that can no longer survive on their home planets.

- Supergirl's family is from Kandor, the Kryptonian city that Brainiac miniaturized and stored inside a bottle.

- Lois Lane's father is General Sam Lane, a military official who doesn't trust Superman.

- Clark Kent's nickname at the *Daily Planet* is "Smallville."

- Lex Luthor remembers Clark Kent from their time together in Smallville, but he doesn't think Clark is important enough to earn his attention.

- Bizarro, Superman's imperfect clone, says "Good-bye" when he means hello and "Hello" when he means good-bye.

- Each member of the Justice League, including Superman, has a special signaling device that alerts him or her when disaster strikes.

- Not all of Superman's enemies have superpowers. Some, like the Toyman or the Prankster, are inventors who build dangerous traps.

Glossary

chronology: A list of events in order of when they happened.

conscience: An inner feeling that acts as a guide to one's good (or bad) behavior.

corps: A group of people or military group doing a particular activity.

exoskeleton: A hard external covering for the body.

extraterrestrial: Someone or something from outside of Earth or its atmosphere.

generations: Sets of family members born and living during the same time.

hologram: A special kind of picture that is made by a laser and looks three-dimensional.

hydraulic: A motor that is operated by a liquid moving in a confined space under pressure.

industry: A group of businesses that provide a particular product or service.

insignia: A badge or sign that shows a person is a member of a particular group or has a particular rank.

journalism: The job of writing news stories for newspapers, websites, television, or radio.

legion: A great number of people.

meteorite: A small body of matter from outer space that makes it to Earth.

radiation: Energy (sometimes harmful) that comes from a source in the form of waves or rays you cannot see.

vault: A secure room or chamber to keep valuables.

128